A camel ride becomes a chase through the desert!

Jessie found herself clinging to the saddle so she wouldn't fall off. The camels drew closer to the running figure. "I'm going to try to get in front of him," their friend Tareq called back over his shoulder. "He'll have to turn back then."

The person turned to run the other way, but he tripped and fell just as Henry caught up to him. Jessie could see Henry grabbing for the thief's bag as the camels drew closer. Tareq and Jessie were only a few feet away when the thief got to his feet and then took off running again...

THE BOXCAR CHILDREN MYSTERIES

THE MYSTERY OF THE WILD PONIES
THE MYSTERY IN THE COMPUTER GAME
THE HONEYBEE MYSTERY
THE MYSTERY AT THE CROOKED HOUSE
THE HOCKEY MYSTERY
THE MYSTERY OF THE MIDNIGHT DOG
THE MYSTERY OF THE SCREECH OWL
THE SUMMER CAMP MYSTERY
THE COPYCAT MYSTERY
THE HAUNTED CLOCK TOWER MYSTERY
THE MYSTERY OF THE TIGER'S EYE
THE DISAPPEARING STAIRCASE MYSTERY
THE MYSTERY ON BLIZZARD MOUNTAIN
THE MYSTERY OF THE SPIDER'S CLUE
THE CANDY FACTORY MYSTERY
THE MYSTERY OF THE MUMMY'S CURSE
THE MYSTERY OF THE STAR RUBY
THE STUFFED BEAR MYSTERY
THE MYSTERY OF ALLIGATOR SWAMP
THE MYSTERY AT SKELETON POINT
THE TATTLETALE MYSTERY
THE COMIC BOOK MYSTERY
THE GREAT SHARK MYSTERY
THE ICE CREAM MYSTERY
THE MIDNIGHT MYSTERY
THE MYSTERY IN THE FORTUNE COOKIE
THE BLACK WIDOW SPIDER MYSTERY
THE RADIO MYSTERY
THE MYSTERY OF THE RUNAWAY GHOST
THE FINDERS KEEPERS MYSTERY
THE MYSTERY OF THE HAUNTED BOXCAR
THE CLUE IN THE CORN MAZE
THE GHOST OF THE CHATTERING BONES
THE SWORD OF THE SILVER KNIGHT
THE GAME STORE MYSTERY
THE MYSTERY OF THE ORPHAN TRAIN
THE VANISHING PASSENGER
THE GIANT YO-YO MYSTERY
THE CREATURE IN OGOPOGO LAKE
THE ROCK 'N' ROLL MYSTERY
THE SECRET OF THE MASK
THE SEATTLE PUZZLE
THE GHOST IN THE FIRST ROW
THE BOX THAT WATCH FOUND
A HORSE NAMED DRAGON

THE GREAT DETECTIVE RACE
THE GHOST AT THE DRIVE-IN MOVIE
THE MYSTERY OF THE TRAVELING TOMATOES
THE SPY GAME
THE DOG-GONE MYSTERY
THE VAMPIRE MYSTERY
SUPERSTAR WATCH
THE SPY IN THE BLEACHERS
THE AMAZING MYSTERY SHOW
THE PUMPKIN HEAD MYSTERY
THE CUPCAKE CAPER
THE CLUE IN THE RECYCLING BIN
MONKEY TROUBLE
THE ZOMBIE PROJECT
THE GREAT TURKEY HEIST
THE GARDEN THIEF
THE BOARDWALK MYSTERY
THE MYSTERY OF THE FALLEN TREASURE
THE RETURN OF THE GRAVEYARD GHOST
THE MYSTERY OF THE STOLEN SNOWBOARD
THE MYSTERY OF THE WILD WEST BANDIT
THE MYSTERY OF THE GRINNING GARGOYLE
THE MYSTERY OF THE SOCCER SNITCH
THE MYSTERY OF THE MISSING POP IDOL
THE MYSTERY OF THE STOLEN DINOSAUR BONES
THE MYSTERY AT THE CALGARY STAMPEDE
THE SLEEPY HOLLOW MYSTERY
THE LEGEND OF THE IRISH CASTLE
THE CELEBRITY CAT CAPER
HIDDEN IN THE HAUNTED SCHOOL
THE ELECTION DAY DILEMMA
JOURNEY ON A RUNAWAY TRAIN
THE CLUE IN THE PAPYRUS SCROLL
THE DETOUR OF THE ELEPHANTS
THE SHACKLETON SABOTAGE
THE KHIPU AND THE FINAL KEY

THE BOXCAR CHILDREN®

CREATED BY
GERTRUDE CHANDLER WARNER

GREAT **2** ADVENTURE

THE CLUE IN THE PAPYRUS SCROLL

STORY BY
DEE GARRETSON AND JM LEE

ILLUSTRATED BY
ANTHONY VanARSDALE

ALBERT WHITMAN & COMPANY
CHICAGO, ILLINOIS

Copyright © 2017 by Albert Whitman & Company
Published in 2017 by Albert Whitman & Company

ISBN 978-0-8075-0698-1 (hardcover)
ISBN 978-0-8075-0699-8 (paperback)

THE BOXCAR CHILDREN® is a registered
trademark of Albert Whitman & Company.

Printed in the United States of America
10 9 8 7 6 5 4 3 2 1 LB 22 21 20 19 18 17

Illustrations by Anthony VanArsdale

Visit the Boxcar Children online at www.boxcarchildren.com.
For more information about Albert Whitman & Company,
visit our website at www.albertwhitman.com.

Contents

A Cat, a Collar, and a Clue

Ten-year-old Violet Alden looked out the plane window as the private jet climbed high in the air. Her sister, Jessie, who was twelve, joined her.

"Good-bye, New Mexico," Jessie said as the desert landscape disappeared beneath the clouds.

"I'm glad we left Anna Argent behind." Violet shivered.

"I'm glad too," Jessie agreed. "She can't get in a plane and chase us." She patted the duffel bag on the seat beside her. "And we have all the artifacts safe in here. We'll deliver them just like we promised the Reddimus Society. Anna won't be able to get them." The Reddimus Society returned stolen art and artifacts to their rightful

1

owners. The head of the society, Mrs. Silverton, who was Grandfather's friend, had asked the Alden children to help them out.

"I can't believe Anna Argent tried to stop our plane from taking off," fourteen-year-old Henry said. Anna had driven a jeep right at their jet as it sat on the runway. A young woman by the name of Christina Keene, who was originally going to deliver the artifacts, had gotten in a jeep to chase after Anna. That meant Christina couldn't get on the plane, and the Aldens had to go in her place. Thanks to the quick action of the Reddimus Society pilots, Mr. Ganert and Emilio, the plane took off before Anna could steal the artifacts.

"Since Anna hid on our train to New Mexico and chased us once we got off there, I'm not surprised," Violet said.

"We're safe now though, aren't we?" six-year-old Benny asked. He didn't like Anna. She had tried to take the pottery turtle they were returning to Acoma Pueblo in New Mexico. It had been stolen from the museum where it belonged, and the Reddimus Society had recovered it.

"We're safe," Jessie assured him. "She can't follow us."

"But where are we going next?" Benny asked.

"You tell us and we'll work out a flight plan," Emilio, the Reddimus Society copilot, said as he opened the refrigerator in the plane's tiny galley. He got out some fruit and cheese and put them on a tray with some crackers. After he set it down on the table in front of Benny, he pointed at the black cat statue that Henry held. "The clue is right here." A messenger had delivered the cat statue right before the plane took off, but there wasn't a note or anything else with it.

"The Reddimus Society asked us to help them because we are good at solving mysteries, so I'm sure we can figure this out," Henry said. The Aldens had been solving mysteries for a long time, ever since they had come to live with their grandfather. After their parents died, the children had been scared to go live with him at first, thinking he might be mean. They had run away and lived in a boxcar in the woods until he found them. He had turned out not to be mean at

all and had even bought the boxcar and put it in their new backyard.

Henry examined the statue more carefully. The cat sat upright staring straight ahead. It was all black except for some gold coloring on the inside of its ears. It also wore a fancy collar that looked more like a necklace. It had rows of red, blue, gold, and black beads strung together to make a broad band. "I'm not sure how this can be a clue." He turned it upside down and inspected the base. "No message written on it that I can see."

Jessie got out her laptop. "Since we figured out how to deliver the turtle by researching that type of art, let's do the same with the cat. We'll see if it matches any pictures." She typed in *cat statue.* Dozens of images appeared on the screen.

"Can I see if I can find any that match?" Benny asked. He liked to play matching games.

"Sure," Jessie said. "Just scroll through them, and show us what you find." She handed the laptop to Benny. It took him only a moment.

"I found one!" he said, excited.

Jessie looked over his shoulder as he pointed at

the screen. "Yes, that one does match. Good job, Benny!"

She clicked on the picture, and some information came up. "Our statue is like the statues they made in ancient Egypt of cats," she told the others. "Cats were worshiped there."

Violet's face fell. "We can't go to ancient Egypt though. There is no such thing as a time-traveling machine."

Henry grinned. "No, but it means we're going to modern-day Egypt. I think one of the artifacts we have to return is Egyptian."

"Egypt is a country, right? Where is it?" Benny knew it was a long way away, but he couldn't remember exactly where.

"It's in the northern part of Africa," Jessie said. "I'll show you on a map." She brought a map of Africa up on the screen and pointed to Egypt.

"Egypt, here we come," Emilio said. "Did you hear that, Mr. Ganert?" he called up to the cockpit.

A cranky voice barked out, "Yes!" The Aldens hadn't known Mr. Ganert for very long, but they had figured out he never seemed to be in a pleasant mood.

"So just like that, you'll take us to Egypt?" Violet asked Emilio.

"That's what we do," Emilio said. He tipped his pilot's hat at her and bowed. "We are at your service, madam."

Violet giggled. Emilio could be very silly. "We don't often have plans too far in advance," he said. "Plus, we don't want to give the Argents time to figure out where we are going. It's a long way though, and we will have to stop at certain points for fuel and other supplies. It should give you plenty to time to figure out where in Egypt we should land. We'll contact Trudy Silverton as soon as you know." Trudy, Mrs. Silverton's granddaughter, worked for the Reddimus Society too. She handled all the travel arrangements and helped the Aldens with anything they needed.

"Right," Henry said. "I forgot about that. Egypt is a big country."

"Yes, it is." Jessie typed in some other search terms into her computer. "This site says it's bigger than Texas and Colorado combined." She read off some other facts. "The main language is

Arabic. Football, or what Americans call soccer, is the most popular sport. Tourists from all over the world travel there to see pyramids and other ancient Egyptian sites and artifacts."

"I hope we get to see pyramids." Benny picked up a piece of cheese and popped it into his mouth. Thinking about pyramids made him hungry.

"Me too," Violet said. "Now we just have to figure out exactly where we are going. I really like the colors in the collar on the statue. Maybe there's a clue underneath it. Does it come off?"

Henry found a clasp. He took the collar off and looked at the back of it. "Nothing here." He handed it to Violet.

"I don't think a real cat would want to wear something so big," Violet said. "But it's very pretty. It could be a bracelet for a person." She wrapped it around her wrist. "If I had made it, I would have kept all the beads in the pattern red, gold, black, blue. I don't know why they broke the pattern with these extra blue beads in different places." She fastened the collar back around the cat's neck.

"You put it on upside down," Benny said.

Violet stared at it. "Are you sure? How do you know?"

Benny pointed at one part of the necklace. "Because those blue beads looked like a backwards C to me before. Now it looks like a C that is facing the right direction." Benny was learning to read and was very interested in letters.

"It does look like a C." Jessie picked up the statue again and traced her finger along the blue beads. "And these other beads that don't follow the pattern look like letters too."

"I see them!" Benny spelled them out. "C...A...I...R...O. Is that a word?"

"Cairo!" Henry said. "It's a city in Egypt."

"That's our clue. Cairo, here we come," Emilio said. "Last time I was there I got to ride a camel. Maybe you will too." He snapped his fingers. "Say, have I got a joke for you. What is a camel's favorite nursery rhyme?" He looked around at all of them, grinning.

When no one could come up with the answer, he shouted, "Humpty Dumpty!" and then broke out in laughter. The Aldens had learned Emilio liked to tell silly jokes, and he liked to laugh at them too.

A loud snorting sound came from the cockpit. "Do you think you could come up here and do some work?" Mr. Ganert called back into the cabin. Emilio made a silly face at the children but then went back into the cockpit.

Benny wished they could go to Egypt without Mr. Ganert. When Benny had first seen him, he thought the man looked like a vampire with his pale skin, thin face, and dark hair that he wore slicked back so that it stuck to his head.

Mr. Ganert also acted like he thought the Aldens couldn't be trusted to work for the Reddimus Society. Benny thought he was probably extra cranky because he had to fly them such a long way.

It was a very long way, even though the plane was comfortable. Emilio showed them how to make the big seats into beds, how to play movies on the television, and how to play music they wanted to hear.

He also showed them his bag of disguises. When they had first seen Emilio on the plane, they hadn't recognized him as the man who had been on the train with them to New Mexico. Jessie was the one who realized it was Emilio under a big fake nose and a wig. Emilio claimed he needed all the disguises to do the work for the Reddimus Society, but the children had talked about it while he was in the cockpit and decided he probably just liked to dress up. It was fun to have him put mustaches and hats and wigs on them. He tried to teach them to speak in different accents, but none of them were very good at it. Mr. Ganert ignored the Aldens most of the time, either staying in the cockpit or sleeping in a seat in the back while Emilio flew the plane.

Benny was pleased they had all the snacks they wanted, but by the time they could finally see the Egyptian desert below them, everyone agreed they were ready to get off the plane.

Benny pressed his face against the window. "There's a huge river down there!"

"That's the Nile," Henry told him. "It's the second-longest river in the world. Only the Amazon River is longer."

"There is a huge city next to the huge river," Violet said. "I didn't know Cairo was so big. The desert here comes right up to the edge of it."

"It's so different than what we saw in New Mexico," Jessie exclaimed. "There aren't any mountains, but there is a lot of sand."

"I see pyramids!" Benny cried.

"Those must be the pyramids at Giza," Jessie said. "I read they were on the outskirts of Cairo."

"Make sure you are buckled up," Emilio called back. "We're coming in for a landing."

The plane landed and then taxied to a stop in front of a long, low building. "Where are all the big planes?" Benny asked.

"This is the terminal for private jets," Emilio said as he came out of the cockpit. "You will be meeting Tricia Silverton, Trudy Silverton's sister."

"You're not coming with us?" Violet asked Emilio.

"No. Mrs. Silverton has another job for us. We need to pick up an important package in Paris as soon as we can. But don't worry. Mrs. Silverton has arranged for someone to meet you and take you through the terminal to meet Tricia."

He went over and opened the door. "Make sure you have everything you need. Take your backpacks and the duffel bag. I don't know where we are taking the Paris package, so it could be a few days before we get back."

Mr. Ganert came out of the cockpit. "Don't lose those artifacts," he warned.

"We won't," Henry said as he picked up the duffel bag.

"Don't let them get damaged either," Mr. Ganert added.

Henry didn't answer. He knew the artifacts were well protected. They were in special boxes that museums used to transport valuable items. The padded boxes kept the artifacts from getting damaged.

A young man in a dark suit wearing an airport badge around his neck was waiting at the bottom of the stairs.

"Hello," he said. "I'm Mr. Khater. Welcome to Egypt. Come this way, please." They followed him into the building where he helped them show their passports to the right people. When they were finished, he walked with them out into an area where drivers were waiting for passengers. Many of the drivers were holding up signs with names on them. None of the signs said Aldens.

"Do you see the person who is to meet you?" Mr. Khater asked. "I was told her name was Tricia Silverton."

"We don't know what Tricia looks like," Violet said.

Mr. Khater frowned. "Oh. Perhaps she will recognize you."

Jessie didn't want to tell him Tricia had never seen the Aldens before.

They waited and the area emptied out as passengers met up with their drivers. When there were only a few people left, a young woman rushed in and scanned the crowd.

"Do you think that's her?" Benny asked.

"I don't think so, but she doesn't look like a driver either," Jessie said. "The drivers are more dressed up." This woman had on white jeans and a black shirt with a big red scarf draped around her shoulders. They heard her speak in another language to one of the few remaining drivers.

"Unless Tricia Silverton is Egyptian, that young lady is not her," Mr. Khater said. "She's speaking Arabic."

They all waited a few more minutes, and no one else entered the waiting area.

"I just realized something," Henry said. "The person we're waiting for will be looking for Christina Keene, not us."

"You're right!" Jessie gasped. "Christina was the one who was supposed to deliver the items!"

"And maybe Tricia sent someone else to meet Christina." Henry said. He looked over at the woman with the red scarf, who was still looking around the waiting area. He walked over to her. "Excuse me. Are you waiting for Christina Keene?"

"Yes," the woman said, looking surprised.

"I'm Henry Alden," he said. "Christina couldn't come. My brother and sisters and I are here in her place." He waved in the direction of where the others stood. "Mrs. Silverton sent us." The others came over and Henry introduced them.

The woman said, "My name is Rania Galal, but you'll have to forgive me. I'm a little confused."

"Could you take us to Tricia?" Jessie asked. "She can explain everything better than we could."

Rania shook her head. "No, I'm sorry I can't. Tricia left Egypt yesterday."

2

Where Is Tricia?

"She...she *left*?" Henry said in disbelief. He looked over at Jessie, whose eyes were wide with surprise.

Rania took her cell phone out of her bag. "Let me make a call. Tricia asked me to pick up Christina because I had to attend in meeting in Cairo. She said she had some urgent matter to take care of. I'll call her." They waited while the woman made the call. When she spoke into the phone, they could tell she was leaving a message. She said, "Tricia, it's me, Rania. There's been a change of plans. Christina isn't here. Some other people named the Aldens are here instead. Give me a call."

She hung up the phone. "I'm not quite sure what to do now."

"We should contact Trudy Silverton," Jessie said. "She might know where her sister went. Do you know Trudy?"

"I've met her," Rania said. "The Galals and the Silvertons have been friends for a long time."

Jessie took out her phone. "Trudy said we could FaceTime with her anytime we needed help."

Jessie made the call and Trudy's face appeared on the screen. Trudy's colorful purple-dyed hair looked like it hadn't been brushed, and her face was strained.

"I'm so glad you called," she said. "I was about to call you. We received a strange message from Tricia. She said she couldn't meet the plane, but she didn't explain why. The message said she'd arranged for other people to help Christina, but she didn't say who."

"Rania Galal is here," Jessie said. "She came to pick up Christina."

Trudy's face brightened. "Oh, that's good to know. Can I speak to her?"

Rania looked over Jessie's shoulder. "Hi Trudy. Tricia asked me to take Christina back to my family's resort. She was in a big hurry and didn't say where she was going. Do you want me to take the Aldens there instead?"

"That would be wonderful," Trudy said. "We're still trying to figure out what to do. It's very upsetting not to know what is going on. It's not like Tricia to take off without telling anyone where she is going. Jessie, until we locate my sister, you'll have to take care of the items without her help. Be very careful who you trust. Go with Rania, and I'll call you again in a few hours. Just watch out for Anna Argent. I have a feeling this has something to do with her."

Violet was alarmed at that. She moved so Trudy could see her. "Anna couldn't follow us to Cairo, could she?"

"You never know what Anna can manage to do," Trudy said. "She's very, very clever."

"We'll be careful," Henry said.

Trudy rubbed her eyes. "Okay, I'll talk to you soon. Thank you, Rania."

After Trudy hung up, Rania asked, "Who is Anna Argent?"

Henry didn't think they were supposed to tell other people about the Reddimus Society, so he said, "She has tried to steal things from the Silvertons."

"Oh, you mean the Reddimus Society," Rania said. Seeing his surprised expression, Rania added, "I know all about it. Don't worry. We've helped them out when we could. I don't think this Anna person will be a problem here though."

The Aldens went with Rania out to her car. She helped them put their luggage in the trunk and then said as they got in the car, "Cairo is a very busy city with quite a lot of traffic. Just sit back and enjoy. It's a long ride."

The city was full of people and cars. Jessie tried to look everywhere at once. "I've never heard so many people honking their horns at once." She wished they could get out and explore, especially some of the markets they passed. People were selling all sorts of things from small stands, including fruits, spices, jewelry, clothing, and rugs.

Violet twisted around and peered out the back window of the car. "At least Anna Argent could never follow us through this, even if she were here."

Benny felt better hearing that. Anna Argent was probably a long way away from them.

Once the car left the city, they drove through many miles of desert and some towns and smaller villages until Rania finally announced, "We are here."

She pulled the car into a driveway that had clumps of palm trees on either side and a sign that read Desert Stars Camp. They drove down the driveway until they reached a big white building with a sign on it that said Lodge. There was another smaller building next to it. In front of that building stood a group of camels drinking water from a round stone trough. An older teenage boy holding the bridle of another camel waved at Rania as they drove by. She passed the lodge and parked the car, gesturing toward some large white canvas tents among more palm trees. They weren't like ordinary camping tents. They were more like small buildings. Each had a big awning over the doorway that shaded a table and chairs placed to one side.

"Some of our guests stay in the lodge, but others

like the experience of a tent in the desert."

"Wow! That sounds like fun!" Benny said.

"I'm glad you think so." Rania stopped the car and opened her door. "My family thought tourists would enjoy experiencing how travelers explored Egypt many years ago. Of course, now all the tents have running water and electricity, so it's not exactly like it was then. The tents even have Wi-Fi."

"That's funny," Jessie said. "I've never heard of Wi-Fi in a tent."

Violet was still thinking about the camels they had passed. "Are the camels friendly?" she asked as they got out of the car. "Can we visit them?"

"You can do more than that," Rania said. "Most visitors enjoy the camel rides. I'll introduce you to my nephew. He is in charge of the camel stables at the moment, when he isn't in school."

"I'd like that job," Violet said.

"Tareq, my nephew, likes it too." Rania went to the back of the car and opened the trunk. "My uncle owns the hotel, and he thinks we should all learn as many parts of the business as possible."

Before they could get their luggage out, a small

yellow van pulled up next to them. The van had an assortment of cakes and pastries painted on it. A man got out and took a white cardboard box out of the back. He said something in Arabic to Rania as he handed her the box.

Rania translated for them. "He's from the bakery in the town near here. He says he has a delivery for Christina Keene. I suppose we'll take the delivery instead." She handed the box to Jessie and then took some money out of her bag. The man accepted the payment, hopped back in the van, and drove away.

Benny had perked up at the word bakery. "Is it time for a snack?" he asked. "It's been a long time since we ate. There is probably something good in that box."

"Why don't we get settled in where we are sleeping, and then we'll open the box," Jessie suggested.

"Right this way," Rania said. "We had planned on Christina staying in the tent at the far end. It's only got two beds in it at the moment, but I'll have some cots brought in."

They took their backpacks and the duffel out of

the trunk of the car and followed Rania into the tent.

It wasn't like any tent they had ever seen. Colorful rugs covered the floor. There were two beds and a few small tables and chairs. A brass camel stood in the corner as a decoration.

"It really is like a hotel," Benny said. "When I saw the tents, I thought there would be sleeping bags."

Rania laughed. "No, our guests wouldn't like that very much. There is even a shower in the bathroom, just through that door in the back. Now, will you be all right for a little while? I need to check with my uncle on some hotel business."

"We're fine," Jessie assured her.

"I'll see you later then." Rania patted Benny on the cheek. "I think Benny wants you to open the bakery box."

After Rania left, Jessie put the box on one of the tables and took the lid off. Inside were rows of small pastries and an envelope with *Christina* written on it. Next to Christina's name was a drawing of an owl.

"That looks like the owl on the Reddimus Society

logo." Henry took out the card Trudy Silverton had given them before they left home. Besides her name and contact information, it had a big decorative R inside a circle made up of swirls. An image of an owl was placed so it looked like it was sitting on top of the letter. It matched the little owl on the envelope.

"It looks like the owls on our flashlights too!" Benny said. Trudy had given all the Aldens flashlights before they had gone on their trip to New Mexico.

"This might give us some answers about where Tricia Silverton went." Jessie opened the envelope. She pulled out a single piece of paper.

"What does it say?" Benny asked.

"It looks like a riddle." Jessie read it out loud.

> I still stand,
> The only one left of the seven.
> Wonders we were.
> Wonder still am I.
> If you can find when I was finished,
> Then you will be able to gaze

The Clue in the Papyrus Scroll

On he who commanded I be built.
From the smallest come the Great.

"That's a hard riddle," Violet said. "Read it again please."

Jessie did. "I don't have any idea what it means. Even if we solve it, I'm not sure what we're supposed to do with the answer."

"Maybe if we had a snack, we could think better," Benny suggested.

Henry picked up the bakery box. "Good idea. I don't know what these are, but I'm sure they are good. You pick first."

Everyone sampled the treats, picking out which ones were their favorites while they discussed the riddle. They were still talking about it when Jessie's phone rang. It was Trudy. Her hair was even more messed up, and she had dark circles under her eyes. "I'm sorry. I haven't found out anything about Tricia," Trudy said. "I'm afraid you'll just have to bring the artifacts back home, and we'll keep them until we have more news."

"Why don't you just tell us where the items

need to go?" Jessie asked. "We can deliver them ourselves, with Emilio and Mr. Ganert's help."

Trudy sighed. "That would be a good idea, except we don't know where they belong or who to return them to. Tricia has all that information. She had filed a report in our computer system, but the file got deleted somehow. I don't understand how that happened. I've been trying to recover the file, but I haven't been able to so far."

"Can't we open the cases up and figure it out ourselves?" Violet asked.

"You won't be able to open the cases. Tricia had them delivered to us already locked up. She's the only one with the security codes. I'm afraid if we tried to break into them, we'd damage the items."

"There are still some things I don't understand," Henry said. "Why did she send them to you in the first place? Why didn't she take them back to where they belong?"

Trudy turned her head away from the screen and said, "I'll be right there." She turned back. "Tricia was planning to deliver them all, but then she got a good lead on a famous stolen painting. She had to follow up on it right away. We haven't heard from her since then. That part isn't so unusual. Tricia has never checked in very often."

Henry picked up the paper with the riddle on it. "I think this might be a clue to at least one of the artifacts. It came addressed to Christina." He read the riddle and then said, "It has to be important."

"I don't know what that means. My sister has always been very good at riddles—too good. Sometimes they are impossible to figure out. I have to go now, but I'll be back in touch when Mr. Ganert and Emilio are back with the plane to pick you up. Bye for now." She hung up the phone.

"We came all the way here, so we can't just give up," Benny said.

"I don't want to give up either. There have to be more clues somewhere." Jessie opened the duffel bag and took out one of the boxes. They had all been wrapped in paper and tied with twine. Emilio had explained they were wrapped that way to disguise that there were valuable items inside. She untied the twine and pulled off the wrapping.

Underneath was a small wooden box. The box was old, the wood worn on the corners.

Next, she unhooked the small brass latch. Inside the wooden box was another box made of hard black plastic. She took it out. It had a keypad lock on it.

"There could be a clue on the case," she said. "Maybe it has something written on it." They examined the case very carefully. It was made of hard black plastic and had a nine-number keypad on a lock holding the box closed. There was nothing written on it.

"Let's compare it to the rest," Henry suggested. "If each box is different, that might be a clue."

They unwrapped all of them and took the cases out of the boxes. All the cases were identical.

Violet picked up one of the wooden boxes they had set aside and opened it up again. She peered inside. "These aren't all exactly alike. Some look older than others. And this one is all marked up on the bottom inside piece. It looks like someone used a marker on it." She pointed to six black dots. "It looks like the pattern you see on dice."

Benny opened another box. "This has dots on it too, but there are only five."

"So the dots could be a clue!" Henry said. "We may be able to figure this out after all."

CHAPTER

3

A Riddle and a Ride

The Aldens opened all the wooden boxes. Each had a different number of dots ranging from two to seven.

"The dots have to be there to tell us which order the items are to be delivered," Jessie said.

"Why isn't there a box with a one on it?" Benny asked.

"Because the clay turtle we took to Acoma Pueblo was item one," Henry reminded him.

Jessie ran her finger over the keypad. "We know the order to open them, but that won't do us much good until we know the codes."

"There were seven items counting the turtle and the riddle says something about seven," Violet said.

"Maybe that means something."

"Maybe," Henry agreed. "I'm going to read the riddle again."

> *I still stand,*
> *The only one left of the seven.*
> *Wonders we were.*
> *Wonder still am I.*
> *If you can find when I was finished,*
> *Then you will be able to gaze*
> *On he who commanded I be built.*
> *From the smallest come the Great.*

"We know one way to figure out riddles is to focus on the words that aren't so common," Jessie said. "*Wonder* isn't such a common word."

Henry repeated a couple of the lines: "*Wonders we were. / Wonder still am I.* The word *wonder* in this riddle means something amazing, not the wonder that means you are trying to figure something out," he said. "What's amazing in Egypt?"

"The pyramids!" Benny shouted.

"Pyramids are amazing, but the riddle says the

wonder is only one of seven," Violet said. "I think there are a lot more pyramids than that in Egypt."

Henry put down the riddle and grinned. "There are more than seven, but I think the seven is something else. We learned in school there were seven wonders of the ancient world. Only the Great Pyramid is still standing of the seven. *I still stand, / The only one left of the seven.*"

"That's it!" Jessie said. "Now we can solve more of the riddle. It says we need to figure out when the wonder was built." Jessie got out her laptop and typed in *Great Pyramid*. She scanned the screen. "It was built in 2560 BC. Try 2560 as the code!"

Henry punched in the numbers. The lock made a slight click and then opened. He lifted the lid, and they all leaned in to see what was inside.

"It's a tiny statue," Benny exclaimed.

"I think it's called a figurine," Violet said.

Benny leaned in to get a closer look then sat back. "I don't see why it's so special. It's a man wearing a hat who is sitting on a chair."

"It looks very, very old," Jessie said. "That's probably what makes it special."

"It has to be a pharaoh," Henry said. "That's not a hat, it's a crown."

"What's a pharaoh?" Benny asked.

"Kings in ancient Egypt were called pharaohs," Henry said.

"That's the rest of the riddle then." Jessie picked up the piece of paper again.

> *Then you will be able to gaze*
> *On he who commanded I be built.*
> *From the smallest come the Great.*

"We just need to know who built the Great Pyramid!" Violet said, excited they were close to solving the riddle.

Jessie went back to her laptop. After a moment, she announced, "A pharaoh named Khufu, who was also called Cheops by some historians. Not much is known about him, but he is very famous because he ordered the Great Pyramid to be built."

They gazed at the tiny figurine again. "Even though we know what it is, we still don't know who to give it to," Violet said.

"Couldn't we just take it to a museum?" Jessie suggested. "I know there is a big museum in Cairo full of artifacts. I read about it on the way here. They could figure out where it goes."

"Let's call Trudy again," Henry said. "She'll want to know we solved the riddle."

Trudy still looked glum when she answered the phone, but a big smile crossed her face after Henry told her they'd been able to open the case.

"I'm so impressed you figured that out!" she cried. "And that you identified the item."

"Can we take it to the museum in Cairo?" Jessie asked.

Trudy shook her head. "Not unless you can figure out the name of the person Tricia worked with on this item. If that person worked in the museum, then you could return it. Otherwise, no. It's a tricky situation with all these artifacts. The museums and other places where the items were stolen from are trying to keep the thefts quiet until they can figure out who stole them. They are afraid the items were stolen by someone who works in the museum, so if we return it to the wrong person, it might disappear again. Do you have any other clues you are still working on?"

"No," Henry said. "That was the only clue."

"We can't do anything else then," Trudy said. "The Reddimus plane will be back in Cairo tomorrow. I'll call Rania and ask her to take you back to the airport. Bring the item and the rest of the artifacts back to us until we know what to do with them. I'll see you soon."

After Trudy hung up the phone, Henry said, "I really wish we could do more."

"Me too. Let's put the figurine away," Jessie said. "I'll feel better if it is locked up again and the cases are put back in the wooden boxes and wrapped up."

"Why don't we mark on the wrappings which box is which," Violet suggested. "We can put little dots on the wrapping that match the ones inside the box."

"Good idea," Henry said.

They had just finished putting the artifacts back in the duffel bag when they heard a voice.

"Hello, Aldens! May I come in?"

An older teenage boy stood in the doorway, the

one they had seen by the camels.

"Hello," Henry said. "Come in."

The boy was tall and lanky and had to duck his head to get in the doorway. His big brown eyes looked just like Rania's. It was easy to tell they were related.

"I'm Tareq Galal," the boy said. "My cousin sent me to see if you wanted to take a camel ride. She has to deal with some hotel business, so she won't be able to see you until later."

"That's nice of you," Jessie said, introducing everyone. "We'd like that. Can we leave our things here? The door to the tent doesn't lock." She was nervous about leaving the duffel bag in the tent.

"Don't worry. Your things will be safe. We have security guards who watch the resort for us. They walk around and keep an eye on things."

Jessie put the duffel bag in the corner and then placed her own backpack in front of it, still worried.

They followed Tareq to the smaller of the two white buildings, which turned out to be the camel stable. The camels all sat in front of the stable, their legs tucked beneath them. All different colors of pom-poms and tassels decorated their bridles. The blankets underneath and on top of the saddles were brightly patterned in shades of red and orange and blue.

"They look like they are all dressed up to go to a party!" Violet said. "What's this tan one's name? Can I pet her?"

"Her name is Al Rahila and yes, you can pet her," Tareq said. "She's very gentle and she likes attention. In fact, they all like attention, but some more than others."

Violet knelt beside the camel. Jessie joined her. "She has such long eyelashes!" Jessie exclaimed.

"Their eyelashes help keep the sand out of their eyes," Tareq explained as he adjusted a blanket on one of the saddles.

"They are really, really big." Benny was a little frightened. Even sitting on the ground, the camels were almost as tall as him.

Tareq moved over to another camel that was a darker brown than the others and checked its saddle. "They're big, but they won't hurt you. Some people think camels are mean. They aren't mean at all if people take care of them. But don't be surprised if they make loud noises. Sometimes they make a growly bellowing noise. It sounds like they are angry. They really aren't. It's like a horse neighing. Don't stand in front of them in case they sneeze on you. Sometimes I think Al Sharif here does it on purpose." As if Al Sharif had understood him, the camel gave a big sneeze. Everyone laughed.

Tareq rolled his eyes at the camel. "Very funny, Al Sharif. Benny, you and Violet can ride together on Al Sharif. He is old and a little slow, but good with children. Jessie, you can ride on Al Rahila. Al Mataya, the other tan one, would be good for

Henry." Tareq patted the neck of a camel that was almost white. "And this is Al Shamlal, my camel. He is light and fast and I'm training him for camel races."

"How fast can they go?" Henry asked.

"Fast, depending on the camel. Not quite as fast as a horse, except when they are running on sand. Their feet are better adapted to it. Our camels don't do much running though, except for Al Shamlal."

"How do we steer?" Benny asked.

"Do you know how to ride a horse?"

"Yes," Benny said. "We all do."

"Use the reins like you would on a horse, but you really don't have to steer. They are used to following Al Shamlal. They will go where he goes." Tareq explained that riders got on camels while the camels were sitting, and the camels then waited for a command to stand up. "Camels get up with their back legs first, so riders tip forward. You'll need to lean back to help keep your balance and then lean forward when they get their front legs up."

Once they were all seated, Tareq taught them the command to get the camels up.

"Whoa, we are really far off the ground," Benny said as his and Violet's camel lumbered up into a standing position. Benny was glad he was riding with Violet.

"A camel's gait is not a smooth as the way a horse walks, so just hold on," Tareq warned when all the camels were up. "They're easy to ride, but it feels strange at first."

Just like Tareq had said, the movements of the camels were very different from those of horses. There was much more swaying back and forth in the saddle than from riding a horse. They spent the next hour out in the desert. As they rode, Tareq told them all about camels and how they were adapted to live in such a dry climate. "Some people think camels store water in their humps, but that's not true at all," he said. "They are able to drink a lot of water at a time so they don't have to drink often."

They rode near a small village and then past it farther into the desert. When they turned back and came within sight of the lodge, Tareq asked, "Would you like to go a little faster?"

"Yes!" Jessie said. Henry agreed.

"How fast exactly?" Benny asked, tightening his hold on Violet.

"Not too fast," Tareq assured him. "As fast as a horse trots, though the way a camel moves, it's more comfortable to ride camels at that speed than it is a horse. It's like they are jogging."

The trip back to the stable didn't take long with the camels moving faster. Jessie had a bad moment where she nearly fell off, but she soon got used to the motion. At the stable, Tareq told them to hold on while the camels lowered themselves to the ground so they could get off.

"You are now camel riders," Tareq declared. "I'm going to feed the camels now, but if you are hungry, there is a buffet set up inside the lodge. Help yourself."

"Yay!" Benny said. The pastries had been very good but not very filling.

"Thank you for taking us on a ride," Jessie said. "Are you coming in to eat?"

"I'll be in soon, but I'll have to eat quickly. I'm taking some of our guests out for a nighttime ride to look at the stars."

They filled up on grilled meat kabobs and bean dishes and a delicious Egyptian flatbread called *aish baladi*, all washed down with fruit juices. After that, many of the lodge's guests went outside to sit around a fire pit while a man who worked at the lodge entertained them with music.

By the time they finished and headed back to their tent, Benny couldn't stop yawning.

Violet noticed and said, "I'm sleepy too."

Henry looked up at the sky. "I see why this place is named Desert Stars. Look at all of them up there. A camel ride at night to watch them would be fun."

"It's nice to be so far away from city lights," Violet said. The only lights they could see were those from the resort and from the village they had seen on their camel ride.

They passed a resort worker who was walking the paths around the tents. He greeted them and then went on his way.

"That must be one of the guards," Jessie said. She was relieved someone had been watching the tents.

Benny walked into the tent first. A motion in

44

the corner caught his eye. It was a hand reaching through a cut in the canvas. The hand took hold of the duffel bag and dragged it through the cut.

"Someone is stealing our bag!" Benny yelled.

Chase through the Desert

Jessie ran in behind Benny. He pointed to the corner. Jessie dashed over and tried to grab the bag. Her fingers closed on one corner, but whoever had hold of it yanked it through the opening.

Henry, who had come in too, yelled, "Outside!" and ran out the door. The rest of the Aldens followed.

At first, it was so dark, no one could see anything, and then Violet shouted, "There!" and pointed at a white shape darting behind another tent. The thief was wearing a long white robe, but there was so little light it was difficult to follow him.

They chased after him anyway, catching glimpses of white as they ran down the paths that wound around the tents. The person veered off toward the back of the resort, heading into the desert. Henry followed and managed to keep up, but he couldn't catch the thief.

Jessie had an idea. "I'm going to get Tareq!" she yelled at Henry. She turned and ran in the direction of the stable. Violet and Benny followed her.

Tareq was taking the saddle off a camel. He looked up, startled at their appearance.

"Tareq! Someone stole our bag!" Jessie yelled. "They ran out into the desert toward the village."

She pointed toward the lights in the distance. They could just make out a figure in a long white robe. Henry was just a dark shape running behind the figure, but Jessie thought he might be gaining on the person.

"Stop, thief!" Tareq yelled, but the thief didn't stop. "No one steals anything from the Galal resort! We'll catch them!"

He jumped back on Al Shamlal.

"Jessie, take Al Rahila," he ordered, pointing at the camel Jessie had ridden earlier. "Benny and Violet, watch the others for me. Come on!"

Jessie barely had time to get on her camel before the animal got up and began to follow Tareq. Tareq urged his camel to go faster, and once it did, Jessie's camel sped up too. Jessie found herself clinging to the saddle so she wouldn't fall off. The camel was moving much faster than the jog they had done earlier in the day.

The camels drew closer to the running figure. "I'm going to try to get in front of him," Tareq called back over his shoulder. "He'll have to turn back then." Al Shamlal sped up even more, so Jessie's camel did too.

The two camels raced toward the village until they were between the village and the thief. The person turned to run the other way, but he tripped and fell just as Henry caught up to him.

As he fell, he bumped into Henry and Henry fell too. Jessie could see Henry grabbing for the bag as the camels drew closer. Tareq and Jessie were only a few feet away when the thief got to his feet and then took off running again.

"Henry, are you all right?" Jessie yelled as the camels reached him.

"I'm fine." Henry stood up and held up the bag so they could see it. "I've got the bag too."

"Should we go after the thief?" Tareq asked.

They hadn't noticed a four-wheel vehicle driving toward them from the village. The driver honked a horn. Jessie's camel was so startled by the noise, it turned and took off jogging back toward the resort. Jessie had just managed to slow the camel when Tareq caught up to her. Henry caught up a moment later, out of breath from running after them.

"The thief got away," Henry said. "He got in the four-wheeler. But at least we have the bag." Henry opened the bag and counted the boxes. "They are all here."

"That's a relief," Jessie said.

"Rania told me Trudy Silverton was worried about the Argent family," Tareq said. "But Rania thought they wouldn't follow you here. We should go back and tell her."

"Yes," Jessie said, "and I am ready to be done with camel riding for the day."

Rania was outside the stable with Benny and Violet as they rode back in. "What happened?" she cried. "I heard yelling and looked out the window to see you racing off into the desert."

Henry explained about the stolen bag and how they'd retrieved it. "The Argents found us here after all."

Tareq began to take the saddles off the camels. "Whoever it was wore Egyptian clothing: a galabia and a turban."

"I know a turban is a hat," Jessie said, "but what is a galabia? Is it the long white robe?"

"Yes, though these days it's not very common, except with older men in smaller villages and with farmers," Tareq explained. "And sometimes people who take tourists on rides and expeditions wear them because the tourists expect it. The person was tall, whoever it was."

"Anna Argent is tall," Benny said. When he had seen her inside the train to New Mexico, she had towered over Violet and him. Benny thought she might even be taller than Grandfather.

"Yes, maybe she wore the robe so no one could recognize her and so people would think she was Egyptian," Henry suggested.

"I don't know who it was, but I wish we knew where to take the artifacts," Jessie said. "I didn't think it would be so hard to keep them safe."

Rania went over to Jessie's camel and showed her how to take the saddle off. "I found something that might help," Rania said. "Tricia left it here, but I didn't know about it until tonight. She gave it to my uncle right as she was leaving. He put it in his office and forgot to tell me. If you come into the lodge with me when we are done, I'll get it for you."

When the camels were all in the stable and everything was put away, they all went into the lodge. Rania brought out a rolled piece of very thick paper from her uncle's office. It had a string tied around it. She handed it to Jessie.

Jessie untied and unrolled it. "It's a scroll."

"Yes," Rania said. "Tourists like to buy these scrolls as souvenirs. They are supposed to look like ancient Egyptian scrolls. They used to write on paper that was made from papyrus plants."

Everyone gathered around to look at the scroll.

"There are little pictures on it," Benny pointed to one. "That's the Reddimus Society owl."

"The one underneath it looks like three pyramids." Violet leaned in closer. "Then the next one is a lady digging, and the one below that is a bird with a worm in its mouth. The last one is a boy with a bow and arrow.

"Yes," Rania said. "They are similar to hieroglyphics, which were the old writing symbols the ancient Egyptians used, but these pictures aren't real hieroglyphics. Look at the woman digging."

"I see what you mean," Jessie said. "That woman doesn't look like an ancient Egyptian. She's got on pants and a shirt with buttons on it. And the boy with the bow and arrow is wearing a tee shirt."

"So it's another puzzle," Henry said. "We just have to figure out what it means."

"I know this kind of puzzle. It's called a pictogram," Tareq told them. "I used to have a puzzle book of pictograms when I was a little boy. You write out the words for the pictures, and that solves the puzzle. I think that woman is supposed to be an archaeologist. That would make sense with the picture of the pyramid."

Jessie asked for a piece of paper and a pencil.

When Rania brought them to her, Jessie wrote out the words *pyramids, archaeologist, bird,* and *bow and arrow.*

Henry looked over her list. "I don't see how those words solve the puzzle. Pyramids and archaeologist go together, but bird and bow and arrow don't."

"That's not just any bird. That's a wren," Jessie said. "Look how its tail is pointed up. Are there wrens in Egypt?"

"If there are, they aren't common," Tareq said. "I don't remember seeing a bird like that."

"It does look like a wren!" Benny said. "Our housekeeper, Mrs. McGregor, put a wren house right outside the kitchen window," he told Tareq and Rania. "She says they eat a lot of bad bugs so she likes them. There is a girl in my class named Wren too. Her parents like birds so they named her after one. She doesn't eat bugs though."

Rania laughed. "I hope not."

"Could Wren be a name?" Violet asked.

"You may be onto something," Henry said. "But I don't see how wren goes with the bow and arrow."

Jessie doodled on the paper, circling the picture

of the person with the bow and arrow. "Instead of bow and arrow, the picture could stand for archer. That can be a name too. Maybe we need to find an archaeologist named Wren Archer." She turned to Rania. "Do you have a computer we can use?"

Rania got her laptop and gave it to Jessie. Jessie did a search and then looked up and smiled. "There is a website for an archaeologist named Wren Archer. It says when she is not teaching, she works near the Great Pyramid. So that's who gets the artifact!"

Everyone was very excited they had solved the puzzle. There were high fives all around.

"Excellent," Rania said. "It's too late to try to reach her tonight, but we can do it tomorrow. There is a government office that oversees all the archaeologists working in Egypt. We can call there in the morning to see if Wren Archer is in Egypt now. If she is, I can take you to her site. I was planning on taking you back to Cairo anyway. Trudy contacted me about the plane coming to pick you up."

"At least we'll be able to return one artifact before

we go home," Henry said. "Anna Argent won't be able to get that one."

"Would you sleep in the lodge tonight?" Rania asked. "I doubt if the thief will come back, but you can move out of the tent if you want to. We have some guest rooms that aren't being used."

The Aldens discussed it and came to a decision together. "No, we'd like to stay in the tent," Jessie said.

"We don't get to sleep in a tent in the desert very often," Violet added.

"We've never slept in a tent in the desert," Benny said.

"I'll put the duffel bag under my bed," Henry said. "And we can pile up all our backpacks around it. If someone tried to sneak in to take the bag, they'd have to move everything first. We'd hear them."

"If you're sure." Rania sounded doubtful.

"We're sure," Jessie said as everyone got up and headed off to bed.

The next morning after breakfast, Jessie got on the phone. She reported what she had discovered. "Dr. Archer is in Egypt conducting excavations near the Great Pyramid. She has a base camp near a site of an ancient workers' village. We can find her there."

They packed their things into Rania's car and said good-bye to Tareq.

"Come back soon," he said. "We'll do more camel riding."

Waving good-bye, everyone settled in the car for the drive back to Cairo. About halfway there, Jessie's phone beeped. "I just got an email from someone named AnOwlFriend," she said

"It has to be someone with the Reddimus Society," Henry said.

"Trudy?" Violet asked.

"The email address doesn't match Trudy's." Jessie opened up the email and read it out loud: "*Be careful who you trust. Many will try to trick you. Ask those who you approach if they are friends of the owls. If they answer 'yes' you know they can be trusted.* That's all it says. There isn't any signature."

"It's a funny email," Benny said. 'It's like in books where you have to know the secret password. *Friends of the owls* is our secret password."

"That's exactly what it is," Henry said. "It's odd though."

"Who would send us that? Do you think it's Tricia?" Violet asked.

"I don't know," Henry said. "Why wouldn't she sign her name? The whole thing is a mystery."

Inside the Great Pyramid

As Rania drove the Aldens into Cairo, the pyramids rose before them. When she parked the car next to a small trailer at the excavation site behind the pyramids, everyone jumped out to stare up at the huge monuments.

"They are incredible," Henry said. "You can't tell how giant they are from the pictures."

"I didn't know they were made up of such big blocks," Violet said. "I thought the pyramids sides were all smooth, but you could climb up these."

Rania shook her head. "People aren't allowed to climb up to the top any longer. Too many people went up and then were afraid to come down. You can only climb up to the entrance. That's about fifty feet up."

Benny held out his arms. "Each block is as big as a refrigerator! I wouldn't like to stack all those."

"I wouldn't either," Jessie agreed. "Just think, they didn't have any trucks or modern equipment to build this."

Violet looked around. "There are a lot of people in white robes here. What if one of them is Anna Argent?"

"Tareq said some of the people who give camel rides wear galabias. I'm sure Anna isn't here," Jessie assured her. "I didn't see anyone following us. I was keeping a lookout in the car."

"I'll keep a tight hold on the duffel bag," Henry added. "I don't think anyone would try to steal a bag from us here. Did you notice all the police-men patrolling on camels? The thief should know now that a camel can catch someone. Let's find Dr. Archer."

"I need to make some phone calls," Rania said. "I'll stay with the car."

Henry walked over to what looked like a group of college students who stood outside the door of the trailer. Their clothes and boots were dusty, and most of them were drinking water from bottles as if they were very thirsty.

"We're looking for Dr. Wren Archer," Henry said. "Do you know her?"

One of the young men pointed at an older woman with curly gray hair standing nearby holding a clipboard and a pencil. The woman's hair stuck out every which way from under the blue scarf tied around her head. She was wearing a pair of glasses but also had two other pairs of glasses attached to strings she wore around her neck.

The Aldens and Rania walked over to her. "Excuse me," Jessie said. "Are you Dr. Archer?"

"I am Dr. Archer." The woman took off her glasses and stared at them, a puzzled expression on her face. "College students must be getting younger and shorter every year, or else I need new glasses." She reached for a different pair and put them on. "You're still looking very young," she said to Rania.

"We're not college students," Henry said. "We're here to return something to you."

The archaeologist continued to stare at them until Jessie remembered the email. "If you are a friend of owls," she added.

Dr. Archer burst into laughter. "I never thought I'd actually hear someone say that. Tricia told me I would, but I didn't believe her. That girl's imagination knows no bounds." She grew serious then. "Do you really have what I think you have? Wait, let's go inside the trailer."

They followed her up the steps and into the trailer, which was packed with papers and computers and pieces of equipment. Henry set the duffel bag down on a table and then took out the box. When he pulled the case out of the box, Dr. Archer clasped her hands together. "I was afraid it was lost forever. Is it undamaged?"

"I think so." Henry punched in the code and opened the lid.

Dr. Archer changed her glasses again. She looked in the case and gasped.

Jessie was worried something was wrong. "It's all right, isn't it?" she asked.

"It's perfect," Dr. Archer said. "I'm so thankful

it's been returned. I will make sure it gets put back in its proper place in the museum where everyone can see it."

It surprised Benny to see how happy Dr. Archer was about the return of the statue. "Can I ask a question?"

"Of course, young man," Dr. Archer replied.

"My sister said the statue was special because it's old," Benny said. "So is everything old special?"

"That is a very good question. Objects as old as this are special, but this one is extra special. We don't know much of anything about Khufu. So much history has been lost. Words were written on things that don't last, or some history was never written down at all. That's why the art and the artifacts that remain are so important. That's where we find the history. Does that make sense?"

Benny nodded.

"Good. I want to get this back to the museum right away, but I expect you would like to stay and look around. Is this your first time in Egypt?"

"Yes," Jessie said. "We're very excited to be here."

"Wonderful. I'll get one of my students to give you a tour."

Dr. Archer closed the case. Henry told her the code, and then Dr. Archer took them back outside and introduced them to the young man they had spoken to earlier.

"This is Ken Kagawa. Ken, will you show our visitors around? It's their first time in Egypt."

"Of course, if you don't mind all the dust coming off me. The wind kicked up when we were working, and the dust coated us." He smiled and ran his hand through his hair. "I usually have black hair, not gray."

"It comes with the profession," Dr. Archer said. "Maybe all that dust is what made my hair gray. Ken, I'll be back in a few hours. Thanks again, friends of the owls." She laughed heartily at that as she walked away.

"If you're ready," Ken said, "we can walk over to the base of the Great Pyramid and talk more there."

"We have a friend with us," Jessie said. "Can we bring her too?"

"Of course. I like having an audience who will

listen when I talk about the pyramids."

Violet ran over and got Rania, and then they followed Ken as he moved through the crowds of people, horses, and camels. When they reached the base, Henry held out his hand and touched one of the giant blocks. "Amazing," he said.

"Most people don't know that it took more than two million blocks of stone to build this."

"Two million is a lot of blocks," Benny said. "I have blocks at home, but not that many."

"If you had that many, it would fill up the whole house," Jessie said, laughing.

"The pyramid is amazing now, but it was even more amazing back when it was first finished," Ken told them. "Back then a final layer was placed on top of this layer. It was made of smaller polished white stones covering the whole pyramid. Just imagine how it looked. It would have gleamed and sparkled in the sun."

"Wow," Violet said. "What happened to the stones?"

"Over time, some fell off due to earthquakes," Ken explained. "Some were carried off for other building projects. A few have been located in some other buildings in Cairo. They were used on some interiors in later construction. Now important historical sites like this are protected from changes, but in the past, people saw old structures as useful sources of building material. Would you like to go inside the pyramid?"

They all said yes except for Rania. She shuddered. "I'll stay outside. I've been in before. It's very stuffy inside."

"Yes, it is," Ken agreed. "Air is pumped in, but it's hard to get enough to make it comfortable. It's also hot, so be prepared," he added. "We have to climb up about fifty feet to get inside. Some people call this the Thieves' Entrance. Robbers cut through here to get inside and steal treasures. Even in ancient times, art and artifacts were lost. That's why we have to protect what is still here."

"It's not very crowded," Violet said. "In fact, it's a little spooky."

"I don't know why there aren't a few more people in here today," Ken said, "though only a few hundred people are allowed each day. Scientists found even people's breaths can cause damage over time. Hard to believe, but breathing gives off too much moisture, and that's bad for the stone!"

The passage was very narrow and steep. It was also not very tall. Ken and Henry had to really bend over to get through. Even Benny had to walk hunched down so his head wouldn't hit the ceiling.

"I can almost imagine people carrying torches through here a long time ago," Jessie said.

"Yes, you can begin to imagine how it was back then, except there wouldn't be electric lights, so it would have been lit by torches."

The passage opened into a bigger space. "This is called the Grand Gallery," Ken said, "though we don't really know what it was used for. The pyramid still has many secrets. There may be new discoveries soon. Archaeologists are using new technology to see if there are hidden chambers still unopened."

"How could there still be hidden places after all this time?" Henry asked.

"We haven't had the technology until recently that allows us to look without damaging what's here. We don't just knock holes in pyramids anymore. Everyone wants to make sure we're not harming something that we may not be able to see."

As Ken was talking, Violet noticed the lights dimmed a little. "What's going on?" she said. Before anyone could answer, the lights went out. It was very, very dark.

"Everybody stand still until they go back on," Ken said. "This happens sometimes."

But the lights didn't go back on. "Someone is walking up the passage," Jessie said. "I hear their footsteps."

"Whoever you are, you should stand still," Ken called. "It's not safe to walk around without the lights. You might fall."

There was no answer. There was also no sound. "I don't hear anyone now," Jessie said.

A tiny beam of light flashed around the room. Everyone jumped. "I knew I'd need my flashlight!" Benny cried. He shone it around on all the startled faces.

"Good job, Benny," Henry said, relief in his voice. "My flashlight is in my backpack in Rania's trunk."

"Mine too," Violet and Jessie said at the same time.

"I've had mine in my pocket just in case." Benny shone the flashlight around the chamber again. The lights came back on.

"Whew," Violet said. "It's no fun to be stuck in a dark pyramid."

Voices came from down the passageway. "Anyone in there?" a man's voice called.

"There are five of us here," Ken yelled back. "We're fine."

"Better come on out," the man said. "Someone has damaged the power cable. We've got a temporary fix rigged, but we need to shut everything down so we can replace it."

"Let's go," Ken said. "I don't know who would damage the cable. If someone thought it was a good prank, it was not."

"I hope it was just a prank," Henry said. He tightened his hold on the duffel bag.

When they came out of the entrance, Rania and one of the Egyptian policemen who had been patrolling on camels stood right outside.

"Anyone else in there?" the policeman asked. They recognized his voice as the one who had been talking to them.

"We don't know," Jessie said. "I thought I heard someone, but we didn't see or hear anyone on the way out."

"Someone put up a sign that the inside was closed temporarily." The man held up a piece of cardboard that someone had written on in marker. "I don't know who did that, but it was unauthorized. It may be the same person who damaged the power cable."

"I don't understand why someone would do that," Rania said.

"I don't know either," the policeman said. "It's never happened before. Were you down below, Miss?" he asked Rania. "Did you see who put up the sign?"

"No, I'm sorry. I wasn't paying attention," she said.

"Very well. You can go now. I need to go in and see if anyone else is still in there," he said. "Be careful on your way down."

When they reached the ground, they were surprised to find Emilio waiting for them.

"There you are. It's time to go," Emilio said. "We've got a long flight ahead of us."

"Thank you for helping us," Jessie said to Rania. "And thank you for the tour," she said to Ken.

"I was happy to help," Rania said. "I'm sorry you have to leave so soon. Come back anytime."

"Yes," Ken said. "If you come back again, I'll take you on a tour of some of the other pyramids. There is always more to see."

"I wish we didn't have to go so soon. I really wanted to help Tricia," Violet said.

"You know Tricia Silverton?" Ken asked. "Any chance any of you are going to see her in Nairobi?"

CHAPTER 6

An Unsettling Accusation

"Nairobi? Where's that?" Benny asked.

"It's in Kenya," Jessie said. She turned to Ken. "You know Tricia Silverton?" she asked.

"Yes, I met Tricia when she came to talk to Dr. Archer two days ago." Ken took out his wallet. "I've been carrying this around since then. She told Dr. Archer to give the necklace to her friend Christina, who would be along in a few days, and to tell the friend she'd gone on to Nairobi. Dr. Archer gave it to me. She said she'd forget about it if she kept it. No one named Christina has shown up, so I don't know what to do with it."

"Christina couldn't come," Violet said.

"That is news about Nairobi," Emilio said. "We

may be going to Kenya next."

Ken held out the necklace. "Will you give this to her?"

Jessie took it. "We'll try," she said.

"Good! Well, it was nice to meet you. I should go back to work."

They all said good-bye, and then Ken headed in the direction of the trailer.

"Let's go back to the plane, and we can contact Trudy and Mrs. Silverton," Emilio said. "I don't know why Tricia would be in Nairobi."

"We're lucky Ken was around when we talked to Dr. Archer. We never would have known where Tricia had gone otherwise," Henry said.

Back at the plane, Mr. Ganert seemed grumpier than ever.

"Are the artifacts safe and undamaged?" he barked at Henry.

Henry set down the duffel bag on the seat. "Yes, they are fine."

"Humph...just make sure they stay that way," Mr. Ganert said as he went back into the cockpit.

They contacted Trudy, but she didn't know why

her sister would be in Nairobi either. "We have several friends and acquaintances there," she said. "I'll make some phone calls while you are in the air. I hope by the time you land I have some leads."

Once they were in flight, Jessie showed Violet and Benny where Kenya was located on a map. "It's south of Egypt, but it's on the eastern part of Africa just like Egypt is." She read them some facts: "Cairo has more people than Nairobi, but Nairobi is still a very big city. The main languages in Kenya are Swahili and English, but there are lots of other languages that people speak too. Many unique African animals live in Kenya, like lions and zebras and giraffes."

"I hope we get to see some animals," Benny said.

"It depends on how long we stay. Don't get your hopes up too high," Henry warned.

Emilio came into the cabin. "I've heard from Trudy. Two friends of the Silvertons saw Tricia yesterday. David Yosei and Harun Kipketer own an art gallery in Nairobi, and they said she was there. I'll go with you to the gallery when we arrive."

By the time they landed, it was getting dark.

They left Mr. Ganert on the plane and went through the airport where was a car waiting to take them to the gallery. Just like Cairo, Nairobi was full of cars and people, though Benny noticed something different. "We aren't in the desert anymore, are we? There are lots of trees here, and it's not so hot."

"Kenya has a different climate than Egypt," Jessie said. "That's why they don't have the same types of animals here that they do in Egypt."

They drove by a park which was full of big trees. Underneath the trees were all different kinds of statues and sculptures. Many people were seated on benches or walking on the paths.

"Here we are," the driver said, pulling up to a building on one side of the park. The sign above the building read, Yosei Gallery. Hanging in the window was a painting of all different colors of dots and a wire sculpture of a person dancing. Light spilled out through the window and they could see the gallery was full of people. "I'll wait in that parking spot over there," the driver said.

As soon as Henry opened the door to the

gallery, they heard the music and the voices of many people all talking at once. People gathered around to look at the artwork on the walls—more paintings of dots—while a trio of musicians played in one corner.

"Do you recognize the owners of the gallery?" Henry asked Emilio.

Emilio scanned the room. "I've met Harun and David once. I think I'll recognize them. Yes, there they are, talking to that older man in the gray suit." He motioned to where two very tall men with dark brown skin standing near a closed door that said Office on it. The men both had their hair cut very short, and one had a short beard. The other didn't. They were dressed up like all the other people in the gallery.

"It looks like we've arrived in the middle of an opening," Emilio said.

"What's that?" Benny asked.

"It's when a gallery shows off an artist's work," Jessie explained. "They have a party the first day of the show. Let's go talk to the owners."

As the Aldens made their way through the

people, Jessie had the strangest feeling that the man in the gray suit with the gallery owners was someone they knew. His back was turned to them, so she couldn't see his face, but there was something familiar about the way he stood.

"David! Harun!" Emilio called out to them.

The man in the gray suit turned at the sound of Emilio's voice.

"Mr. Carter! What are you doing here?" Henry said. The Aldens had met John Carter on one of their mystery cases when Mr. Carter was working for the FBI. Later, Mr. Carter had done some work for Grandfather and had helped the Aldens with some other mysteries. The Aldens remembered how he'd always been able to solve problems. Jessie remembered he had always been very kind and ready to smile.

He wasn't smiling now. Henry introduced Emilio to him, and in turn Emilio introduced the Aldens to David and Harun.

Mr. Carter said, "Mrs. Silverton asked me to come to Kenya. A valuable wood carving was stolen from the National Museum of Kenya. Tricia Silverton was seen looking at it on security camera footage before it went missing. The police think she stole it. Mrs. Silverton wants me to look into the case."

"I can't believe it!" Violet cried.

"Me either," Jessie said. "From what we know about Tricia, she wouldn't steal anything, especially not art! She spends her time returning stolen art."

"That's what we have been telling Mr. Carter," David said.

"Didn't you have a theft from your own gallery?" Mr. Carter asked. "I saw the police report."

Harun frowned. "Yes, but that was the day before Tricia arrived. She couldn't have had anything to do with that. She would never steal from us."

"Why would a thief steal your art? It isn't old," Benny said.

David and Harun both smiled. "Art doesn't have to be old to be valuable," David explained. "Art made last year can be valuable too. It depends on the artist and how well that person can make art that means something to those who look at it."

As more people came into the gallery, the noise grew louder. "Let's step into our office so we don't have to shout," Harun said.

Once inside, Harun shut the door. "Can I ask why you and your young friends are here?" he said to Emilio.

"We are trying to locate Tricia," Emilio replied. "She hasn't been in touch with her sister for several days."

"That's odd," David said, "though Tricia was acting a bit oddly while she was here. Not like she was planning on stealing anything though."

"Odd how?" Mr. Carter asked.

"She was in a hurry and wouldn't say why. Talking about things like mysteries and passwords and such." David and Harun looked at each other and then back at the Aldens as if they were expecting one of them to say something.

Jessie realized what they were waiting for. "We like owls," she blurted out. "Do you? I mean, are you friends of owls?"

Both Harun and David relaxed. "Yes! We like owls too," Harun said. "Tricia told us to wait for someone to say that, but we didn't expect it to be four young persons. So that means you are the ones to hear the riddle. Let's see if I can remember it all. It goes like this:

> *Some called me king of this place.*
> *Was I? That I will not say.*
> *Though much of its history is yet to be uncovered,*
> *The stones stand while the sun rises and sets.*
> *Find when the king's treasures were discovered,*
> *And that will reveal one of them to you.*
> *But all kings in the end*
> *Trade diamond and gold for a leafy crown.*

"I need to write that down," Jessie said. "I can't remember all those lines."

David gave her a piece of paper and a pencil. Harun repeated the riddle. "I hope you know what it means," he said, "because I don't."

"We don't either," Violet said. "We'll have to work on it."

"I'm not sure what we are supposed to do next," Henry said.

"Perhaps you can solve the riddle at your hotel," David suggested. "It's a lovely place."

"We didn't know we had a hotel here," Violet said.

David checked his watch. "Oh I thought you knew. Tricia told us she made a reservation at the Giraffe Inn for the person who heard the riddle. It's a place she stays whenever she is in Nairobi. You are in for a treat."

"Are there giraffes there?" Benny asked.

"There certainly are. The hotel is right in the middle of an animal reserve. A herd of giraffes visits each morning and evening hoping for treats."

"That sounds amazing," Henry said.

"Did Tricia happen to mention anything that might give us a clue where she's gone?" Mr. Carter asked.

David shook his head. "No, she said she had several places she needed to go, but she didn't mention any specific cities or countries."

"She did say something that was a bit strange though." Harun paused as if he were trying to remember. "She said she'll be going where all roads go."

"That doesn't make much sense," Jessie said.

"That's all we know." Harun motioned to the door. "I'm sorry, but we have to get back to our guests."

They all went back into the gallery, and Harun and David said good-bye before moving into the crowd to greet people.

Mr. Carter walked out the front door with the Aldens and Emilio. "I'm on my way to Paris," he said as he handed Jessie a card. "If you hear from Tricia Silverton, please call me. We need to get this straightened out as soon as possible."

Jessie nodded and then Mr. Carter waved down a taxi and jumped in.

"I'm staying with some friends," Emilio said. "I'll get a taxi. The driver will take you to your hotel. I don't know exactly what is going on, but Tricia obviously has some sort of plan. I expect there will be a message for you at your hotel. Call me as soon as you figure out where we need to go next, and then I'll contact Mr. Ganert and Trudy."

The Aldens got back in the car. "I'm ready to be at a hotel," Violet said. She could tell it was getting late. "The plane is nice, but another hotel will be nice too."

"I'm ready to see giraffes!" Benny cried.

"We'll be there soon," the driver said.

It wasn't long before the car turned into a lane that was bordered on either side by a grove of trees. The lane wound around until the car pulled up in front of a big stone mansion covered with ivy.

"This looks like another great hotel," Henry said.

"What were those?" Violet cried. "Pigs with fur?" Two small animals ran across the lawn and around the corner of the house.

"Those are warthogs," the driver said. "I've heard some live here with the giraffes."

A woman came out the front door and down the steps. She had on an apron. Her red hair was pulled back in a ponytail, but both her hair and her face looked like they had flour on them. When the Aldens got out of the car she said, "Welcome to Giraffe Inn. I'm Alexandra Goodwin, the manager, but everyone calls me Alex." She looked down at her apron. "Oh dear, forgive me. I forgot I had this on. I like to do a bit of baking when the chefs will let me in the kitchen. We've been waiting for you."

As they got their luggage out of the trunk and

the others talked to the manager, Henry realized something odd about what Alex had said. "Weren't you expecting Christina Keene?" he asked.

"I was, until someone left a message earlier today that four young Aldens would be arriving in her place." She smiled. "And here you are!"

Henry looked at the others. Jessie said, "Do you know who left the message?"

"No, the person who answered the phone didn't take down that information. I expect it was Tricia Silverton. She made the reservation for Christina in the first place. Would you like to see your room?"

"Where are the giraffes?" Benny asked.

"We have a big parcel of land for them to roam on, so we don't see them all the time," Alex explained. "You'll definitely see them at breakfast though. They like their treats. Your room is right this way."

"Were there any messages for us?" Jessie asked. As happy as she was for all of them to stay at a beautiful hotel, they needed more clues if they were going to solve the riddle and figure out where to go next.

An Unsettling Accusation

"No, no messages," Alex replied. "If you'll follow me, I'll show you upstairs."

Not an Owl but a Crow

Alex took them upstairs and opened the door. "We've put you in a suite so you'll have plenty of room."

Violet admired all the old polished furniture and the colorful rugs. "It looks like we're staying in someone's house instead of a hotel," she said. "It's all very pretty."

Alex smiled. "That's how we want our guests to feel. Call the front desk if you need anything. In the morning, come down for breakfast whenever you are ready. The giraffes will be waiting for you. If you don't need anything else, I'll say good night."

After the manager left, Henry said, "Tricia must

have left the message that we were coming instead of Christina. How did she know?"

"Do you think she called Trudy and Trudy told her?" Violet asked.

"I don't know. Wouldn't Trudy have told us or contacted Emilio? It's all very strange," Henry said.

Benny gave a giant yawn. "I'm going to bed so I can wake up and see giraffes."

"Good idea," Jessie said. "We can work on the riddle tomorrow."

Jessie woke up first. She got up and went to the window. When she looked outside, she jumped back, startled. She looked again and then smiled. Opening the window, she called, "Benny, Violet, come see."

Benny and Violet scrambled out of bed. Henry followed. At the window, a tall giraffe stood inches away, peering curiously at them.

"It's so tall!" Benny said. "We're way up on the second floor."

"It's beautiful!" Violet said. "I'm sorry we don't have any food for you."

The giraffe dipped its head as if it were sorry too,

and then it moved to peer into another window. Other giraffes were approaching the hotel.

Benny tried to imitate their stately gait. Everyone laughed watching him. "You need longer legs," Jessie teased.

"I'll do it better when I'm as tall as Henry," Benny said.

"Let's go to breakfast," Violet said. "I think they are coming to eat."

Downstairs in the breakfast room, a huge buffet filled a table along one wall. Benny could hardly believe all the pastries and fruit and other dishes full of all types of food.

A waiter dressed in a white jacket and a bow tie came in and opened the rows of tall glass doors that led out to a terrace. As soon as they were all open, a giraffe stuck its head in. Everyone laughed. Two more came up and put their heads in as well. A shy smaller one hung back, watching.

Alex came in and said hello. "Do the giraffes eat pastries too?" Benny asked her.

"No, we feed them special pellets made up of dried grass, corn, and molasses." She opened a

cabinet and took out several metal bowls full of pellets. "If you'd like to feed them, go ahead and take a bowl."

They all did, feeding each of the bigger giraffes. "I never noticed before, but giraffe faces are kind of like camel faces," Henry said.

"They both have long eyelashes," Jessie said.

Violet asked if she could try to feed the shyer one. Alex said she could and then added, "Her name is Violet."

"That's my name too!"

"Then she should like you," Alex said. "Let's go meet her."

Outside, Violet and Alex walked slowly up to the young giraffe. Violet held out her bowl. The giraffe came forward and dipped her head in, scooping up the pellets, bit by bit. When the giraffe had emptied the bowl, it nudged Violet's head.

"She wants to be petted," Alex told Violet.

Violet reached out her hand and gently petted the giraffe's neck. "She's so soft!"

"She is, and she's a pretty girl too. After you eat, why don't you come back out and sit on the terrace.

You might have some other visitors then."

After breakfast everyone spent the next few hours out in the garden with the giraffes. The warthogs came to visit too, as well as the hotel dog, who was named Snuffles. "She tries to make the same snuffly sound the warthogs make," Alex explained, "because she thinks she's a warthog." Eventually the animals wandered off, heading across the wide lawn. "Feel free to walk around and explore," Alex said when she saw Violet's disappointed face. "We have over a hundred species of birds on the property. I have to do some paperwork in my office, but I'll see you later."

Alex went inside but then came right back out. "A letter was just delivered for you. Maybe this is the message you were waiting for last night." She handed an envelope to Jessie before going back inside.

Jessie was about to open it when Benny pointed at it, "There is something written on it. Right there in the corner."

"It's a little drawing of an owl!" Violet said.

"Then it's definitely from Tricia," Jessie said, excited for a new clue.

The Clue in the Papyrus Scroll

Violet picked up the paper and unfolded it. "And this is another riddle!" She read it out loud.

> A *clever man he was,*
> *Who knew jigsaw puzzles would be loved by many.*
> *If you visit the country from whence he came,*
> *You will be one step closer to completing your task.*

She read it again and then said, "It doesn't say figure out who invented jigsaw puzzles. I don't know what this means: *Who knew jigsaw puzzles would be loved by many.*"

"We'll have to research jigsaw puzzles. I'll be right back." Jessie ran upstairs and got her laptop, bringing it back down to the terrace. She searched through some sites and then said, "Jigsaw puzzles were first made popular by a man named John Spilsbury. He lived in England. The riddle makes sense then: *A clever man he was, / Who knew jigsaw puzzles would be loved by many.*"

"*If you visit the country from whence he came, / You will be one step closer to completing your task,*" Henry read. "Our next stop is England."

"Yay!" Benny said. "I love England."

"Me too. But we don't know where to go once we are in England." Violet pointed out.

"I'll call Emilio," Henry said. When Emilio picked up the phone, Henry explained the clue and how they had solved it. "So we know it's England, but that's all we know."

He listened for a minute and then told the others what Emilio had said. "He thinks we will get more information soon, or at least before we arrive in England. Since it's about a ten-hour flight, he wants to leave early in the morning. We're to stay here for another night."

"That means we get to feed the giraffes again!" Benny said.

"Yes," Jessie said, though she was worried that they still didn't have any idea how to solve the riddle about the king.

They spent the rest of the day at the hotel exploring and watching the animals. Snuffles followed them everywhere, bringing them sticks until they understood she wanted to play fetch. They learned all the giraffes' names and helped name some of the baby warthogs. Violet declared she had decided that baby warthogs were as cute as baby pigs. Dinner was served in a big dining room by candlelight. Alex explained, "We don't have electricity in this room on purpose, so people can experience what it would have been like when this house was first built."

As much as they enjoyed the day, Jessie kept waiting for a message, but none came.

By bedtime, Henry brought up that they still hadn't received a new clue. "I wonder if there was a mix-up, like Dr. Archer giving the necklace to Ken instead of keeping it to give to Christina."

"I think it will come in the morning," Violet said.

She was right. As soon as they were finished with breakfast and had brought their bags down, Alex came out of her office. "Your driver is here," she said. "And we've gotten another message for you." She held out a piece of paper. "This one was phoned in to us. The desk clerk wrote it down. It doesn't make sense to me, but maybe it does to you."

Jessie took it. "It says, *Beware. Sometimes an owl is not an owl, but a crow instead. And we all know crows like to steal shiny objects. Who is the crow?*"

"That's very strange," Henry said. "We'll have to think about that."

The driver came in the front door. "I'm sorry to rush you," he said, "but I'm supposed to get you to the airport as soon as possible."

"I hope you can come back and visit sometime," Alex said.

"We will," Henry assured her. The others nodded and said their good-byes. Benny waved at the giraffes as they drove away.

Once they were on the main road, Henry said, "Would you read the message again?"

Jessie did and Benny said, "Crows do like shiny things, but how can an owl be a crow?"

"I think it means someone working for the Reddimus Society is really a thief," Henry said. "The message says crows like to steal shiny things. Maybe Tricia did steal something from the museum."

Jessie shook her head. "It's too hard to believe. Why would Tricia take the time to make arrangements for Christina to stay at such a nice hotel if Tricia was busy planning on stealing something?"

"We need to find out who left the messages,"

Violet said. "If it wasn't Emilio or Trudy or Mr. Ganert, who would it be?"

"Let's call Trudy," Benny said. "She might know."

Jessie dialed Trudy's number. She listened and then said, "There's no answer, just a message to leave a message."

"We'll have to wait until we get on the plane to ask," Henry said. "Emilio might know."

Mr. Ganert was waiting impatiently for them when they arrived at the airport. "We should have been in the air an hour ago," he scolded. "Where is that Emilio? He's never on time." He looked out the window, grumbling under his breath. When he turned to go back to the cockpit, he pointed at a package laying on one of the seats. "Someone delivered that for you."

Jessie picked up the package. "There's a little drawing of an owl on it," she said as she unwrapped it. Inside was a cloth bag with a drawstring. She opened it. "It's a big bag of puzzle pieces. So that's why we got the riddle about the jigsaw puzzle."

Violet took the bag from Jessie and looked in. "This looks like a hard puzzle. There are lots and lots of pieces in here." She reached in and took out a handful.

"They're tiny pieces," Benny said. "Like the big puzzles we all do together at home that have thousands and thousands of pieces."

Jessie laughed. "Maybe not thousands and thousands, but there may be at least one or two thousand for this puzzle. Is there anything besides puzzle pieces in the bag? It will be extra hard if there isn't a picture of what the puzzle looks like when it is finished."

Violet looked again. "There's nothing else in here."

"Here comes Emilio," Henry said. They looked out the window. The copilot came dashing out of the terminal carrying some bags. A man followed behind him carrying more. When the two got to the plane, Emilio called out, "Anyone up there? I need some help. Someone take these and put them in the galley. No one will go hungry on this trip."

Mr. Ganert came out of the cockpit as the children went to help. "Just put the bags in the storage area and shut the door," he ordered. "You can put things away after we take off. Let's move."

Everyone rushed to get the bags secured, get in their seats, and put on their seatbelts.

They had just buckled in as the plane rolled down the runway and took off. "I'm getting used to this," Violet said, "though I miss our boxcar."

"I do too," Benny said.

"Our boxcar will still be there when we get home, though I miss it too. And Watch and Grandfather and Mrs. McGregor." The seatbelt light went off, so Jessie unfolded the table between the two sets of seats. "I think we should work on the puzzle first and then the riddle. What do you think?"

Everyone agreed the puzzle was the place to start. "Let's make a plan," Henry said. "Benny, you are good at finding the edge pieces, so that's your job. The rest of us can start sorting by color."

As soon as they started sorting, Violet said, "All these pieces have writing on them." She held up one piece. "This one has a *C* and an *O* on it." She picked up another piece. "And this one has a *D* and a *U* on it."

"You're right! It has to be another clue!" Jessie

said. "We'll put it all together and then figure out how to flip it over to read the back."

They got to work. Emilio checked on them every so often. They also remembered to ask Emilio about the messages sent to the hotel.

"It wasn't me," he said. "And Mr. Ganert never has anything to do with those sorts of details. I'll ask Trudy when I contact her again." He sat down and tried to fit a puzzle piece into the right place. When he found it, he shouted, "I did it!" He leaned back and put his hands behind his head. "Say, do you want to hear a puzzle joke? What did the alien say to the jigsaw puzzle?" he asked, his eyes lit up with glee.

When no one could answer, Emilio cried, "I come in piece and you come in pieces! Get it? 'I come in piece, P...I...E...C...E' instead of 'I come in peace!' That's a good one." He burst into laughter. He was enjoying himself so much, everyone else laughed too.

"I get it," Violet said. She explained it to Benny.

"That's funny," Benny said, still giggling. He repeated the joke so he could remember to tell it to Grandfather.

The Clue in the Papyrus Scroll

Henry leaned down to look more closely at the section where Emilio had put a piece. "I know what this is. No wonder it's all gray and green. It's one of the most famous sites in England."

The Giant's Dance

"Tell us!" Benny said.

"It's a place called Stonehenge," Henry explained.

"You're right!" Jessie said. "I remember seeing a picture of it."

"That's a funny name for a place," Violet said. "What is it?"

Jessie took out her notebook and drew some shapes on it. "It's an amazing monument made of giant stones. They're placed in a big circle like this." She tapped her pencil on the drawing and then drew a bit more. "Some of the stones are topped with other giant stones. It's very, very old, and no one is sure why it was built. It's hard to draw exactly. Let's finish the puzzle. Then you can see what it looks like."

Henry fit another piece of the puzzle into place. "And we need to see what is written on the back. The sooner we finish the puzzle, the better."

"I'll leave you to it," Emilio said. "Mr. Ganert and I will figure out the closest airport and notify Trudy so she can make some arrangements for us."

Everyone kept working. When they got hungry, Jessie helped Emilio get out some of the food that he'd brought aboard. There were plenty of snacks, and later in the day he set out food for dinner. They ate quickly so they could get back to the puzzle.

Eventually, Violet said, "There must be some more edge pieces, Benny. We should have that part all put together by now."

"There aren't," Benny said. "I looked all through the pieces three times."

"Let's look one more time," Jessie suggested. "Sometimes it's easy to miss them."

All four of them looked but couldn't find any. "That's a bad sign," Henry said. "If there are edge pieces missing, there might be inside pieces missing too."

When the last piece fit into place, it was clear the pieces for the bottom right corner of the puzzle were missing. "I hope the clue on the back is all there," Jessie said. "I hope it was written in the middle of the puzzle."

"Let's turn it over and see," Henry reached for the puzzle.

"It will all fall apart if we move it!" Violet said.

"We can slide it onto one of the trays in the galley," Jessie suggested. "And then use another tray to help us flip it over."

It took all four of them to slide the puzzle onto the tray and then turn it over.

"Does it say anything?" Benny asked eagerly.

"It just looks like lots and lots of letters," Violet said. The back of the puzzle was filled with rows of random letters. "Is it really a clue?"

"It's a word search puzzle," Henry said, "the kind where you have to look in either the rows or the columns or diagonally to find the hidden words."

"You're right! I see a word!" Violet said, running her finger across the middle of the puzzle. "This spells out 'DOCTOR.'"

The rest of the words took much longer to find. "Remember we need to look at diagonal words and even words spelled backward," Henry said. Eventually, they found only three words: DOCTOR, MUSEUM, and DOUGLAS.

"I think there were some important words in the part that's missing," Violet said.

That isn't much of a clue," Jessie agreed. "The last message was about Dr. Archer, so this one might be about a Dr. Douglas. And he must work at a museum." Jessie got out her laptop and read through some information. "There are a lot of archaeologists named Douglas."

"See if any of them work at Stonehenge," Henry said.

Jessie tried a few different words. "Nothing comes up in a search."

"What if Douglas is a first name?" Benny asked.

"Good thinking, Benny. Let me look some more." After several minutes, Jessie sat back and sighed. "There are a lot of archaeologists who have Douglas as a first name too, but I can't find one who works at Stonehenge. I don't think I'm searching the right way, and there is so much information."

"I'll try," Henry said. He didn't have any luck either. After several minutes he closed the laptop. "There is a museum close to Stonehenge in a nearby town. I suppose we can go there first and ask if a Dr. Douglas has anything to do with the museum."

"That's a good plan," Jessie said. "Maybe we can at least figure out the riddle and open the case."

Jessie read it again:

> *Some called me king of this place.*
> *Was I? That I will not say.*
> *Though much of its history is yet to be uncovered,*
> *The stones stand while the sun rises and sets.*
> *Find when the king's treasures were discovered,*
> *And that will reveal one of them to you.*
> *But all kings in the end*
> *Trade diamond and gold for a leafy crown.*

"*Some called me king of this place,*" Jessie repeated. "Was there a king of Stonehenge?"

"I've never heard of that," Henry said. "Let's look

it up." Jessie gave him her laptop. "I'll just type in *king of Stonehenge*" he said, "and we will see what comes up."

He had to look through several sites to find what they needed. "In 1808 archaeologists discovered an ancient burial site three miles from Stonehenge. It was full of gold and bronze treasures. People thought the treasures must have belonged to a king, and because the site was close to Stonehenge, they came up with the King of Stonehenge name. Since then, other burial sites have been called that, but this one, called Bush Barrow, had the most valuable treasures."

"So 1808 has to be the code to the case," Jessie said. "*Find when the king's treasures were discovered, / And that will reveal one of them to you.* The 'when' is 1808."

"Try it!" Benny cried, bouncing up and down in his seat with excitement.

Henry took the case marked with three dots out of the bag. "Jessie, it's your turn to open one."

Jessie put in the code. The lock clicked open. Inside the case was a small diamond-shaped gold disk. Its burnished surface almost glowed.

"I didn't know something so old could be so shiny. What is it?" Benny asked, leaning over to see.

"Maybe it's a piece of jewelry," Violet suggested.

"Or maybe it fell off of something bigger, like some sort of vase or box," Jessie said.

"I don't know what it is," Henry said, "but if we find Dr. Douglas, he'll be able to tell us."

Emilio came out of the cockpit to look at the artifact. "We'll be landing soon at an airport not too far from Stonehenge. I hope you can figure out where this goes."

Violet looked out the window as the plane taxied to a stop. "There's someone waiting for us. Two people, someone dressed like an airport worker, and...and....Mrs. McGregor!"

Their housekeeper waved. The Aldens all waved back, eager for Emilio to open the door. When he did, everyone rushed down the steps. Mrs. McGregor hugged them all.

"We didn't expect to see you," Jessie said.

"Your grandfather sent me to see how you were

doing," Mrs. McGregor said. "I've been concerned after we heard Tricia Silverton wasn't traveling with you. As soon as we knew you were coming to England, I hopped on a plane and here I am."

"We've been fine," Henry said. "We've seen some amazing sites and stayed in some fantastic hotels."

"And we fed giraffes!" Violet said.

"We rode camels too." Benny added.

"That does sound like fun," Mrs. McGregor said, giving Benny an extra hug. "I want to hear all about it, but we should let this man check your passports and then we can go." Mrs. McGregor gestured at the airport worker who stood next to her.

After the man was finished with the paperwork, Emilio, who had gotten off the plane with Mr. Ganert, said, "Let me know if you can find the right person and if you get a message telling us where to go next."

Mr. Ganert mumbled something about hating last-minute trips, and then without saying good-bye to the Aldens, he got back on the plane.

As the Aldens and Mrs. McGregor walked out to the parking lot, Mrs. McGregor said, "The driver who picked me up in London after my flight is waiting for us. Do you know where we need to go?"

Jessie explained about the museum, and once they got in the car, the driver told them he knew the way.

The car wound around the narrow roads. Violet looked out the back window. "There is a car behind us," she said. "It's been there ever since we left the airport."

Jessie turned around to look too. "It's probably just a car going in the same direction as us."

"Yes, it can't be Anna Argent, or any other Argents," Henry said. "They can't know where we are. We didn't know we were coming to England until last night. The only other people who know we're here are Trudy, Mrs. Silverton, Emilio, and Mr. Ganert."

"Your grandfather and I knew," Mrs. McGregor reminded them. "But the Argents couldn't find out from us."

The children spent the trip telling Mrs. McGregor everything they had done until the driver let them out in front of the museum. The car that had been behind them didn't stop. It went past and disappeared. Violet was relieved.

They went inside to a woman who sat at a ticket counter. "We're looking for a Dr. Douglas," Jessie said. "Does he work here?"

The woman shook her head. "No, I'm sorry. We don't have anyone here by that name."

"We're stuck then," Violet said. "What do we do now?"

"Wait, I just thought of something. Remember Benny's idea about Douglas being a first name?" Henry went back to the desk and asked the woman if anyone there had a first name of Douglas.

Once again she said, "I'm sorry. We don't."

"Thank you." Disappointed, Henry turned to walk away.

"Wait," the woman called. He turned back around. "I'd forgotten. Dr. Brown goes by a first name of Grant, but Grant is actually his middle name. He goes by D. Grant Brown, because his father is an archaeologist too, another Douglas Brown. Does that help?"

"Yes!" Violet cried.

"Is Dr. Brown here?" Jessie asked.

"Dr. Brown does some research here, but he's not in the museum at the moment. He is out at Stonehenge with a group of visitors giving them a tour."

"Is he coming back here after the tour?" Henry asked.

The woman shook her head. "No, we are having a reception here tonight. Dr. Brown hates parties. I believe he is going home after the tour."

"We'll go to Stonehenge then and try to find him," Henry said.

"We have something very important to give him," Violet added.

"Let me call the visitor center then," the woman said. "I'll have them hold the proper tickets for you, the ones Dr. Brown and his group are using. Those are the ones that allow visitors to walk among the stones at sunset. Other times of the day you have to look at the stones from a pathway." She made the call and then told the Aldens, "It's all arranged. You should hurry though. The site closes soon."

The Aldens started to rush out the door. Jessie

stopped and turned back to the woman at the desk. "How will we recognize Dr. Brown?"

The woman laughed. "You'll know him, or at least you'll hear him. He's a tall man who talks in a loud voice, and he talks a lot. If for some reason he's not talking, you can recognize him by his jacket. He always wears it. It's brown with a fuzzy white collar that looks like mice have been chewing on it. His wife keeps throwing it away, and he keeps rescuing it from the rubbish bin."

"It shouldn't be too hard to find someone like that," Henry said.

The driver was waiting for them and took them straight to the visitor center. They jumped out just in time to see a group of people getting on a tram. Henry ran up to the window and explained who they were. The woman at the window gave him the tickets and said, "Hurry, you'll just make the last tram."

On board the tram, they watched as the vehicle went around a curve and they could finally see the circle of stones.

"They're giant!" Benny cried.

"They didn't look so big in the puzzle," Violet added.

"Some people used to call Stonehenge the Giant's Dance, because they thought only giants could have built it," Henry told them. The stones rose out of the ground in the middle of a huge grassy field. Their dark gray color made them stand out against the bright blue sky.

"They are a little spooky," Benny said. Violet nodded her head in agreement.

As they got out, Jessie said, "That must be Dr. Brown." She pointed to big, tall man striding over the field toward the stones as the group of people behind him scurried to keep up.

Henry said, "Let's catch up to him, and then we can talk to him when he's done giving his tour."

They caught up and stood at the back of the group. Dr. Brown was waving his arms around enthusiastically. "Fantastic, don't you think?" his voice boomed. "Think what a great effort it must have been to lift these massive stones into place, all without the use of modern equipment." He went over to one and stood looking up at it. "Astounding!"

he continued. "It also took tremendous effort to get the stones here. These kinds of stones are only found miles away. It must have taken hundreds of people to move them."

A woman in the group raised her hand. Dr. Brown said, "What's your question? Speak up!"

"Why was it built?"

The big man grinned. "It's a mystery and one I've devoted my life to solving. I'm having a grand time working on it. All we know is that the reason must have been very important. There are many, many theories, but nothing we can prove. I wish we had written records from when it was built, but we don't. That's why it's called a prehistoric monument. For those of you who don't know, 'prehistoric' means before recorded history. Here's another fact for you. Many people don't know that there are standing stones all over Great Britain, Ireland, and Northern France. Some are just a single stone and some are in groups. Stonehenge is the most famous because it is so large and so many of the stones are still standing."

Other people asked questions and Dr. Brown answered them all, striding back and forth in front of the stones waving his arms around the whole time. When there were no more questions, he said, "The tram will take you back to the visitor's center. I'm going to stay a bit and walk back."

The group moved off. Jessie walked up to the archaeologist. When he saw her, he said, "If you have another question, I'll be happy to answer it, but you'll have to hurry. You don't want to miss the tram. It's more than a mile back to walk it."

The Clue in the Papyrus Scroll

"I don't have a question. Well actually I do, but not about Stonehenge. Are you a friend of the owls?"

CHAPTER 9

A Brush with the Enemy

The man looked at her with the same puzzled expression Dr. Archer had worn when they had approached her. He also had the same reaction to Jessie's question, bursting into a loud laugh. "I certainly am." He looked around eagerly at them. "Does this mean it's been found?"

"We do have something for you, but we don't know what it is." Henry took the case out and handed it to Dr. Brown. "The code is 1808."

Dr. Brown put in the code and then lifted the lid carefully. "Oh," he said as he looked inside, "it is a rare beauty, even for such a wee thing. I'll be glad to see it back where it belongs."

"What is it?" Violet asked.

"That is a good question," Dr. Brown said. "We're not exactly sure, though it was some sort of decoration either worn by a person or placed on a weapon. It was found at a burial site near here along with some other artifacts. We don't know the name of the person buried there, but he must have been very important because of the gold found with him."

"How can that little piece of gold be important enough for someone to want to steal it? Did they want it because it was made out of gold?"

"Not necessarily. While gold is valuable, this is far more valuable because of its age. We know so little about Stonehenge that everything we find from the time period it was built in is very important."

"That's what Dr. Archer said about old things found near the Great Pyramid," Benny told him.

"Dr. Archer is right, whoever they are," Dr. Brown said. "I want to get this back to the museum. Since you've come a long way to bring this to me, would you like a quick tour of the museum?" He laughed. "If you haven't discovered it already, I love to lecture."

A Brush with the Enemy

Their car followed him in his car back to the museum. When they got out and joined him at the entrance, he was frowning. "All these cars in the parking lot! I forgot about the reception. We'll just go in and keep to ourselves. Maybe no one will notice us."

Henry thought it would be difficult for Dr. Brown to go unnoticed anywhere, but he didn't say anything. They followed the archaeologist inside. He carried the case very carefully in two hands as if he was afraid he'd drop it.

The rooms were crowded with people who were standing around talking in small groups. It was very noisy. "This is not a good time for a tour," Dr. Brown told the Aldens and Mrs. McGregor. "If you can come back tomorrow morning, I can show you around without all this foolishness. They aren't even looking at the displays!"

Dr. Brown took them to a display case in the corner where there was an empty stand and a sign that read, "Bush Barrow Lozenge."

"What's a lozenge?" Violet asked. "I thought that was a cough drop."

"That's one meaning," Dr. Brown said as he put in a code on a lock on the side of the display case. "It also can refer to something that is diamond shaped, like our little treasure."

He punched in the code on the case holding the gold piece, opened it up, pulled out the lozenge, and set it on top of the case. Just as he went to open the door of the display case, a women yelled, "I see a rat! It's right there! Look out, don't step on it!"

Some people screamed, and excited voices filled the museum. Everyone started moving around, looking down at the floor for the rat.

All of the sudden, Dr. Brown yelled "Stop!" and then Benny felt someone bump into him. The person pushed past him and into the crowd. He just caught a glimpse of tall woman with a blond ponytail.

"Someone grabbed the case! It's gone!" Dr. Brown shouted, so loud everyone except the woman froze. She was still moving, and because everyone else was still, she darted around them easily and out the door.

"Stop her!" Dr. Brown yelled again, but that

BUSH BARROW LOZENGE

turned out to be a mistake. Everyone moved then, crowding toward the door so no one could get out very quickly.

By the time the Aldens and Dr. Brown made it out to the parking lot, the woman was nowhere in sight.

"It was Anna Argent," Benny said. "I saw her. She looked just like she looked on the train."

They went back inside. "I'll call the police," Dr. Brown said. "I can't believe that just happened."

The rest of the guests were asked to leave, and the Aldens and Mrs. McGregor stood waiting for Dr. Brown to finish his call.

"I can't believe Anna Argent found us," Henry said.

"I can't either," Jessie said. "Violet, you must have been right about someone following us."

Violet wasn't listening. She had caught sight of something on the floor by the edge of a display that gleamed against the carpet. Running over to it, she picked it up. "It's the lozenge!" she cried.

Dr. Brown heard her. He hurried over and she gave it to him. Wonderful!" he said. "It must have fallen out when that woman grabbed the case. Thank you, young lady! You have sharp eyes."

He opened the display, placed the lozenge on its stand, and then closed and locked the case. "There. It will be safe now. We've upgraded our alarm system since the theft. I need to go call the police again and tell them they are no longer needed. Thank you again."

The Aldens said good-bye to Dr. Brown, relieved they had managed to deliver the third artifact safely. "Is it time to eat now?" Benny asked.

"It is," Mrs. McGregor said. The driver took them first to a restaurant for dinner and then after that followed Mrs. McGregor's directions. She showed him where to turn in at a lane with a sign that read, Danby Bed and Breakfast.

"Here we are," the driver said as he pulled up in front of a farmhouse at the end of the lane.

"Can you drive around to the side of the house?" Mrs. McGregor asked him. "We are in a cottage next to the main house."

He did and when the headlights lit up the cottage, Violet said, "It looks like a cottage from a fairy tale!" The little stone cottage had a thatched roof and an old wooden door. Next to the door stood a clay pot full of daffodils.

"I like it," Benny said, "even though there aren't going to be giraffes at breakfast."

"I have the key," Mrs. McGregor said. "I checked in earlier before I came to meet you."

It was warm and cozy inside. Everyone put their things down. Henry lit a fire in the fireplace, and Mrs. McGregor made them some hot chocolate.

When they were settled around the fire, Jessie said, "I wish we could figure out where Tricia is. What she said about roads has to be a clue, but I don't know how we'd figure it out."

"What did she say?" Mrs. McGregor asked.

"She said she was going where all roads go. We don't know any place like that."

Mrs. McGregor laughed. "I think I do. There is an old saying, 'All roads lead to Rome.' I suspect Tricia Silverton went to Rome."

"Do all roads really lead to Rome?" Benny asked and then tried to answer his own question. "They can't because the ones in the United States don't.

They can't go under or over the ocean."

"No, but back when the Roman Empire covered most of Europe, the Romans built many roads that really did lead to Rome," Mrs. McGregor explained. "There were older roads that led to other places, but the saying has stuck ever since then."

"Let's FaceTime Trudy," Jessie suggested.

When Trudy heard what Mrs. McGregor had told them, a big smile crossed her face. "You're right. She probably did go to Rome. She's got a small apartment there because she is in the city so much. I'll give you the address, and once you arrive you can go there and ask her landlady if she has seen her. I almost forgot! What about the artifact?"

Jessie explained everything. "Terrific!" Trudy said. "You are all doing a great job. I feel like we are close to figuring out what Tricia is doing and getting the rest of those artifacts back where they belong. Anna Argent should realize by now that she is not going to outsmart you. I'll call Emilio and let him know the plans."

It was arranged that they would leave for Rome the next morning, and Mrs. McGregor was to go with them. On the plane, Mr. Ganert was his usual grumpy self. Emilio was not in a happy mood either. He didn't tell any jokes or ask any questions about their adventure the day before.

"What do you think is wrong with Emilio?" Violet whispered as the plane took off.

"I don't know," Jessie said. "Maybe he's just tired of being around Mr. Ganert all the time. That wouldn't make me happy either."

When the plane landed in Rome, there was a call from Trudy. Her happy expression from the night before was gone. "There's been a change of plans," she told them. "Mr. Carter is meeting you at the airport. Go with him and then call me later."

"What does he want with us?" Henry asked.

"He didn't say, just that it was important." Trudy hung up before they could ask more questions.

Mr. Carter was waiting for them. As they came down the stairs, they could see his expression. He was not happy.

Where All Roads Lead

Mr. Carter greeted Mrs. McGregor and then turned to the children. "There is someone who wants to talk to you."

"Who?" Henry asked.

"Inspector Donati," Mr. Carter said. "He's with a special division of the Italian police, the Carabinieri Art Squad. Their job is to recover stolen art."

"Why does he want to talk to us?" Jessie asked. She hadn't imagined that would be the reason they were meeting Mr. Carter.

"It's best if I let him tell you. This way."

As they drove into Rome, Jessie tried to admire the beautiful buildings, but she was too worried about why they were going to see a policeman.

She could tell Violet and Henry were worried too. Benny, at least, was not. He pointed out all the statues they passed. "This doesn't look anything like Connecticut!" he kept saying at every statue.

At the Art Squad's headquarters, an assistant showed them into a tiny office. There was barely enough room for all of them. "Mr. Donati will be with you shortly," the woman said as she left.

Not only was the office tiny but it was also full of stacks of paper and crammed with file cabinets. Perched on every surface were small clay sculptures, though it wasn't clear what they were supposed to represent. Violet leaned in close to look at one on the very edge of the desk. "I think this one might be a person's head. This could be the nose and this might be a mustache." She pointed at some of the lumpier bits on the sculptures.

"This one has a mustache too," Henry said, examining another.

The door opened and a man in a dark suit and shiny dress shoes walked in. He wasn't much taller than Henry. "Agent Carter, hello," the man said and then smiled at the Aldens and Mrs. McGregor.

Agent Carter introduced them. "I see you are admiring my son's work." Mr. Donati picked up one of the clay pieces. "He wants to be a sculptor. I sit for him, and then he gives me all the practice busts he makes. I think he shows talent, though he always makes my mustache much too large." Mr. Donati patted his own small, trimmed mustache. "But we are not here to talk about my son." He grew serious. "We have had some disturbing news from Paris."

Taking a folder off his desk, he opened it, pulling out a photograph. "Tricia Silverton was seen on the street outside this auction house in Paris right before a valuable ruby ring was discovered to be missing." The blurry picture showed a woman in a purple hat and a big coat walking down the street. The woman had on large sunglasses and a scarf around the lower part of her face.

"How can you tell who that is?" Jessie asked. "You can't see much of her face at all."

"We know it's her. An employee recognized her when she came in to make an inquiry."

Henry remembered something. "Emilio and Mr. Ganert went to Paris while we were in Cairo."

"Yes, the Reddimus Society pilots were supposed to pick up the ring after the auction house determined it had been stolen from the owner in England. It appears Tricia Silverton got there first."

"Tricia wouldn't steal a ring!" Violet said.

"I didn't know you had met her," Mr. Carter said.

"We haven't, but I just know she wouldn't do anything like that." Violet looked at her sister and her brothers. "Right?"

"Violet is right," Jessie said. "No one in the Silverton family would steal anything."

"Why don't you tell me everything that has happened so far," Inspector Donati said. "We understand you have had some mysterious messages."

It took some time, but between the four of them, the Aldens managed to explain everything that had happened.

"Most unusual," Inspector Donati said when they finished. "I think it is best if you continue on as you have been doing. If you receive more clues from Tricia, please contact me. If you can't reach me, contact Mr. Carter. We need to clear this up."

Henry said, "We will. I'm sure Tricia didn't do anything."

Inspector Donati said good-bye to them and showed them out. Once they were outside the building, Violet asked, "What do we do now?"

"You'll have to wait until someone, who I hope is Tricia Silverton, delivers a clue to you," Mr. Carter said. "I expect it will be soon. Mrs. Silverton has arranged for you to stay at the hotel the Silvertons always use in Rome." He took a card out of his wallet. "It's called the Villa Torretta. Here's the address. Would you like me to get a taxi for you?"

"Yes, thank you," said Mrs. McGregor.

After he flagged down a taxi for them and they were seated inside it, he leaned in the window and said, "I have to go back to London, but I will be in touch with Trudy Silverton. Good luck."

The taxi took them on several busy roads full of more beautiful buildings until it pulled up in front of one with a garden all around it. The Villa Torretta," the taxi driver said.

"It doesn't look like a regular hotel. It looks like a big house, even bigger than the one in Kenya,"

Benny said.

"I'm sure it's called Villa Torretta because it used to be someone's house," Mrs. McGregor said. "A villa can be like a mansion."

A doorman opened the door for them. They walked into a lobby of gleaming woodwork and sparkly chandeliers. The man at the front desk checked them in and then motioned for a bellhop to show them to their rooms.

As they walked to the elevator, the bellhop said, "If you are friends of the Silvertons, I'm sure you will enjoy some of the artwork here." He motioned to all the paintings, tapestries, and other decorations that filled the lobby. Upstairs, he opened the door to their suite and then said, "Enjoy your stay."

After he had gone, Violet said, "Can we go sightseeing since we don't have any clues?"

"Yes!" Benny said. "Where should we go first?"

"I know a little about Rome," Mrs. McGregor said. "My sister and I came here on vacation a few years ago. I know the first thing you have to do in Rome is get gelato."

"What's gelato?" Benny asked.

Mrs. McGregor smiled. "You'll like it. It's ice cream."

Benny grinned. "Let's go!"

Mrs. McGregor asked at the front desk, and the man behind it directed them to the nearest gelato shop. "It's right down the hill near the Trevi Fountain," he said. "Don't forget to throw coins in the fountain."

Mrs. McGregor said, "We won't. I did last time I was here, and see, it worked!"

As they left the hotel, Jessie asked, "What did the man mean by that?"

"The Trevi Fountain is one of the most famous fountains in Rome," Mrs. McGregor explained. "There is a legend that if you throw a coin in the fountain, you will return to Rome someday. We'll get our gelato and then walk over to the fountain so you can see it."

The gelato shop had dozens of flavors in all different colors. "It's like rainbows of ice cream," Violet said. "But I've never heard of some of these flavors."

"The fun part of eating gelato is to try something new," Mrs. McGregor said.

Violet knew what she wanted right away. She chose almond. The rest took longer to make up their minds. While they were deciding, Violet walked over to the window so she could watch the people. Crowds of people filled the sidewalks. She caught sight of a woman in a purple hat walking away from the shop. The woman disappeared into the crowd. She didn't have on a coat like they'd seen in the picture, and Violet couldn't see her face, but she had the strangest feeling it was Tricia Silverton.

She hurried back over to the others and told them what she had seen. "Tricia might be here after all," Jessie said. "Maybe she will contact us at the hotel."

"She might," Mrs. McGregor said. "We'll go back as soon as you've seen the fountain. Have you decided on a flavor, Benny?" After much discussion, Benny chose the chocolate hazelnut gelato, and Jessie and Mrs. McGregor picked melon. Henry decided to try fig.

They walked to the fountain as they ate. Everyone agreed the gelato was delicious.

Jessie gasped when the fountain came into view. "When you said we were going to see a fountain, I didn't think it would be anything like this."

"It's almost as big as a swimming pool!" Benny said.

The fountain stood right in front of a building and took up almost one whole side of it. Water spilled into the pool from all different parts of the giant sculptures that lined the edge of the fountain. In the center was a shell-shaped chariot and strange creatures that looked like winged horses that were part fish. There were statues of bearded men trying to hold on to the horse creatures. Henry thought it was incredible.

"I love everything about it," Violet said, "but I really love the turquoise color of the water. I wish I could try to paint it."

"It's beautiful, isn't it? We'll all throw coins in the fountain." Mrs. McGregor took some coins out of her purse. "You're supposed to stand with your back to the fountain and throw the coin over your

left shoulder."

They all took turns, and after watching the fountain for a little longer, they decided they should get back to the hotel.

As soon as they walked in, the bellhop hurried over. "A messenger just delivered this," he said. He handed Henry a package wrapped in brown paper. It was addressed to the Aldens, and there was the same little drawing of an owl.

"We should wait until we are up in our room to open it," Henry said, glancing around the lobby. He didn't think any of the people there were working for the Argents, but it was better to be safe than sorry.

Benny could hardly wait to see. As soon as they were in the room, he said, "Let's see what's inside! I want to know where we are going next."

Jessie unwrapped the package. Inside were a bag of wooden stamps, an ink pad, and an envelope.

Violet opened the bag and looked at the stamps. "These are alphabet stamps. Wait, not all of them." She pulled out one. "This one is a dragon."

"A dragon," Henry repeated. "I wonder what that means?"

The Clue in the Papyrus Scroll

Jessie smiled. "We'll find out soon enough, won't we?"

Turn the page to read
a sneak preview of

THE DETOUR
OF THE ELEPHANTS

The third book of
the Boxcar Children
Great Adventure!

The Aldens continue their mission to return lost
artifacts around the world by visiting the Great
Wall of China, but halfway around the world
trouble seems closer than ever!

After breakfast, the Aldens met Cousin Joe, Cousin Alice, and Soo Lee in the hotel lobby. Henry called their driver, Mary, to tell her they were ready to be picked up.

"How long will it take to get to that village? Mutan...something?" Benny asked.

The hotel clerk overheard Benny. "Do you mean Mutianyu by the Great Wall?" she asked.

Benny nodded.

"It's not far," the woman said. "About one and a half hours from Beijing."

Jessie wished Benny hadn't asked. There was no one else in the lobby besides the clerk, but the Aldens' last riddle said to be careful who they trusted. Jessie had not even told Mary their plans. It wasn't until she arrived in the van that she learned where they would be driving.

"Oh, you'll have fun at the Great Wall!" Mary

exclaimed. "I'm glad you're getting to see some sites."

Everyone was quiet on the ride except for Benny and Soo Lee, who were trying to think of names for the cloth tigers they had been given the day before.

When Mary pulled into a parking lot and announced they had arrived, Benny said, "I don't see a wall."

Mary laughed. "You'll see it when you get out and look up."

Everyone jumped out of the van. The wall was far above them, way up on top of a steep slope. Benny's mouth dropped open. "It looks a lot bigger than it did on the poster!"

"In many places, the wall was built to run across the tops of mountain ridges," Mary explained. "That made it even more difficult for invaders to cross."

"I'll be waiting down here when you've seen everything," she continued. "I'm going to go get some coffee and read a book I brought. Take as much time as you need."

Everyone got their camera cases and Henry took their duffel bag as well. They walked through the parking lot and into an area where people were selling souvenirs, hats, and arts and crafts.

"There's a sign for Mutianyu Village," Henry said. "I hope it's not very big. I don't know how we are supposed to find Dr. Zhang there."

The village wasn't very large. They walked around looking at some of the older buildings until they saw a sign with both Chinese characters and English words on it. The English part read, "Mutianyu Guest House and Restaurant."

"Let's go ask there," Jessie suggested.

Inside they found a woman at a reception desk working on a laptop. She looked up and smiled. "Can I help you? I'm afraid we have no rooms available, but our restaurant is open."

"We are looking for someone," Henry said. "Someone named Dr. Zhang. Do you know her? Or him? We don't know if Dr. Zhang is a man or a woman."

"Yes, of course," the woman responded. "Dr. Zhang is a woman. She is staying here while she works on a book, but today she is on top of the wall, showing a group of visiting students around."

"We'd like to see her as soon as possible," Jessie said. "Would we be able to find her if we went to the top of the wall?"

"Yes, unless you pass her coming down as you go up. She'll be with a large group of young people. She is about this lady and gentleman's age," the woman said smiling at Cousin Joe and Cousin Alice. "Dr. Zhang carries a cane with her, though she doesn't use it all the time. It has a silver dragon head for a handle. You should be able to recognize that."

"What is the best way to get to the top?" Henry asked. "Is there a path?"

"There is but it's quite a long ways to the top. It's about four thousand steps and will take you more than an hour to hike. If you want to get up more quickly, there is a cable car you can ride."

"Let's take the cable car," Violet said. "That sounds like fun."

"Yes," Jessie said. "I'd like to find Dr. Zhang as soon as we can."

The woman from the guesthouse told them how to find the ticket booth for the cable car. They bought tickets and went to wait in line.

"These look like cable cars at ski resorts," Benny said as he watched the bright orange cars go up the mountain. "I didn't know they used cable cars other places."

"It's a good way to get up high," Jessie said. "And since they are all enclosed, people can go up and down even in bad weather."

The platform they were waiting on was very crowded. "Stay close," Jessie said to the others. "We don't want to get separated." They inched their way forward as the people in front of them got into cars. When it was the children's turn, the operator asked how many were in their group. Cousin Joe replied, "Seven."

"You'll need two cars then," the man said. He directed Joe, Alice, and Soo Lee to one. "The rest of you can go up in the next one." Joe, Alice, and Soo Lee got into their car, and Soo Lee waved good-bye through the window.

The next cable car came up the platform and the man directed the children inside. Jessie, Benny, and Violet were already in when someone on the platform behind Henry yelled, "Watch out!" Henry stumbled forward into the car, but a person outside the car reached in and took hold of the strap on the duffel bag. Henry tried to grab it back, but the bag was yanked off Henry's shoulder as the door closed. "Wait!" Henry yelled, but the car was already moving away from the station. Their duffel bag was gone...

Want to Add to Your Boxcar Children Collection?

Start with the Boxcar Children Bookshelf!
Includes the first twelve books, a bookmark with
complete title checklist, and a poster with activities.

978-0-8075-0855-8 · $59.99

And keep solving mysteries with
new titles in the series added each year!

HC 978-0-8075-0705-6
PB 978-0-8075-0706-3

HC 978-0-8075-0711-7
PB 978-0-8075-0712-4

HC 978-0-8075-0718-6
PB 978-0-8075-0719-3

HC 978-0-8075-0721-6
PB 978-0-8075-0722-3

Hardcover $15.99 · Paperback $5.99

GERTRUDE CHANDLER WARNER discovered when she was teaching that many readers who like an exciting story could find no books that were both easy and fun to read. She decided to try to meet this need, and her first book, *The Boxcar Children*, quickly proved she had succeeded.

Miss Warner drew on her own experiences to write the mystery. As a child she spent hours watching trains go by on the tracks opposite her family home. She often dreamed about what it would be like to set up housekeeping in a caboose or freight car—the situation the Alden children find themselves in.

While the mystery element is central to each of Miss Warner's books, she never thought of them as strictly juvenile mysteries. She liked to stress the Aldens' independence and resourcefulness and their solid New England devotion to using up and making do. The Aldens go about most of their adventures with as little adult supervision as possible—something else that delights young readers.

Miss Warner lived in Putnam, Connecticut, until her death in 1979. During her lifetime, she received hundreds of letters from girls and boys telling her how much they liked her books.